CHOOSE YOUR OWN ADVENTURE®

CRYPTID CHRONICLES
MOTHMAN

BY CRISTIN BISHARA

ILLUSTRATED BY SOFIA CAVALLARI
COVER ILLUSTRATED BY SOFIA CAVALLARI

CHOOSECO®
WAITSFIELD, VERMONT

Illustrated by Gabhor Utomo
Cover illustrated by Brian Anderson
Cover design by Dot Greene
Layout and typesetting by Peter Holm

For information regarding permission, write to:

CHOOSECO
P.O. Box 46
Waitsfield, Vermont 05673
www.cyoa.com

Publisher's Cataloging-in-Publication Data
Names: Bishara, Cristin, author. | Cavallari, Sofia, illustrator.
Title: Cryptid chronicles: Mothman / by Cristin Bishara ; illustrated by Sofia Cavallari.
Description: Waitsfield, VT : Chooseco, 2025. | Includes 40 b&w illustrations. | Audience: Ages 9-12. | Summary: In this interactive adventure, the reader has moved into their grandfather's abandoned house and discovered his secret research into aliens and cryptids, including the Mothman. Depending on your choices, you might investigate the myth of the Mothman, travel through time, discover secret government facilities, or be transported to distant worlds.
Identifiers: ISBN 9781933390710 (softcover)
Subjects: LCSH: Mothman – Juvenile fiction. | Extraterrestrial beings – Juvenile fiction. | Time travel – Juvenile fiction. | Conspiracy theories – Juvenile fiction. | Point Pleasant (W. Va.) – Juvenile fiction. | LCGFT: Plot-your-own stories. | BISAC: JUVENILE FICTION / Action & Adventure / General. | JUVENILE FICTION / Science Fiction / General. | JUVENILE FICTION / Interactive Adventures.
Classification: LCC PZ7.1 B57 2025 | DDC [Fic]--dc22

Published simultaneously in the United States and Canada

ISBN: 978-1-933390-71-0

Printed in Canada

The authorized representative in the EU for product safety and compliance is EUCompliance Partner, Pärnu mnt. 139b – 14, 11317 Tallinn, Estonia, www.eucompliancepartner.com

11 10 9 8 7 6 5 4 3 2

BEWARE and WARNING!

This book is different from other books.

YOU and you alone are in charge of what happens in this story.

There are dangers, choices, adventures, and consequences. YOU must use all of your numerous talents and much of your enormous intelligence. The wrong decision could end in disaster—even death. But don't despair. At any time, YOU can go back and make another choice, alter the path of your story, and change its result.

After your grandfather disappears under mysterious circumstances, YOU and your family move to his old abandoned house, and it isn't long before you encounter his secret research on aliens, cryptids, and other world-shaking conspiracies. All of it seems so far-fetched . . . but what if your grandfather's theories aren't so out-there after all? What if the Mothman is closer and more terrifying than you ever imagined? What if an alien threat really does loom ever closer?

YOU alone, and the choices you make, will save—or doom—the world!

Fear grips you as you gaze up at your grandfather's abandoned house. It's an old Victorian mansion, three stories tall, nestled above the Ohio River on the West Virginia side. The foothills of the ancient Appalachian Mountains rise behind its broken windows and slate roof like a dark shadow. You scale the termite-eaten steps. The rotten porch groans under your weight. As you open the creaking door and cross the threshold, the feeling of dread in your chest deepens.

There's something strange here, you just know it.

Turn to the next page.

2

You hear your parents in the kitchen, unpacking boxes, chatting happily about their renovation plans, oblivious to the heavy feeling in the air. Your grandfather was an odd man who believed in strange creatures and UFOs. After he disappeared two years ago, the house sat vacant until he was presumed dead, though his body was never found. The inheritance was finally sorted out, and now this is your home.

Go on to the next page.

A chill runs down your spine at the thought. You try to reason with yourself. This will be a spectacular house once it's all fixed up. There's nothing to be afraid of! You decide that if you bravely explore, room by room, closet by stairway, you will find there's nothing at all out of the ordinary.

Turn to the next page.

Your parents' voices fade as you climb the spiral staircase to the second floor, then head down a dim hallway. Overhead, a chandelier is covered with dust and spiderwebs. You flip the switch on the wall, but it doesn't work. Beneath your feet is a faded, thin carpet. The walls are decorated with dark oil paintings. There's not a single door along the entire long hallway, which seems odd. It's a dead end.

But then, retracing your steps, you feel a cold draft. You pause. And then you see it. Camouflaged in the middle of an oil painting of a black moth with piercing red eyes, there's a small doorknob! Your breath catches in your throat. A hidden room? Tentatively, you touch the knob and suddenly feel dizzy. A nagging sense of unease makes you waver. At the same moment, you notice the warning sign that's hung directly below the moth painting.

PRIVATE!
Do Not DARE Enter!

If you decide to heed the warning for now and investigate another part of the house, turn to page 12.

If you stick with your plan to bravely explore, turn the doorknob, and go to page 72.

PRIVATE!!
DO NOT DARE ENTER!

6

As you sprint past a sign that says *Shaft 76,* your foot connects with something hard, sending it clattering down the tunnel. "Shh!" you hiss at the object as it stops beneath a dangling lightbulb, bathing it in an eerie glow.

A skull!

You recoil with horror. The long jaw and shape of its teeth tell you it must have been a mule. Poor thing. Your dad mentioned once that mules worked alongside men—and *kids*—in the mines, before there were laws against child labor. You shiver, hoping you don't come across any human remains.

Go on to the next page.

"This way!" a soldier shouts. Your blood runs cold. You've given yourself away making too much noise! Their pounding footsteps echo against the low ceilings and uneven walls, dynamited and chiseled by miners a century ago.

Frantically, you look around at the wooden boxes labeled EXPLOSIVES, broken antique lanterns, and pairs of dirty old boots. Just ahead is a wooden mine cart. Its metal wheels and the train track underneath are rusted, but it's your only hope. You jump inside and unlock the brake.

Turn to the next page.

8

Slowly, you inch forward. At this rate, the troops will catch up.

Go! Faster!

You get your wish. The track drops suddenly. Racing downhill, you grip the sides of the cart. The rough wood is full of splinters, which painfully gouge into your hands. There are no more lightbulbs. It's pitch-black, and the air is damp and freezing. As you fly around a curve, the cart tips sideways onto two wheels! Teeth rattling, you lean the other way and the cart crashes back down onto the track. When you grab the brake, the wooden handle breaks off. You're careening out of control on a wild roller coaster ride, plunging into the bowels of the earth.

Go on to the next page.

Despite the terrible danger, though, you oddly start to feel sleepy. It's getting hard to breathe. Vaguely, hazily, you remember Dad mentioning *blackdamp*. Something about West Virginia mining, how toxic gases naturally release from coal. You should have thought of this sooner, before you climbed inside the cart.

Your head dips, and you groggily lie down, gradually succumbing to the fumes. When the cart veers off the old track and plummets into the void, you're already unconscious. You feel nothing as the frail cart explodes upon impact, shattering into a thousand pieces.

Someday, far off in the future, when human remains are indeed discovered deep inside the mine shaft, they are yours.

The End

You realize it's a shrine to your grandfather's obsession with UFOs and creatures like Bigfoot and the Loch Ness Monster, and especially something called the Mothman. You take in the cluttered tables. Scribbled in his shaky old handwriting, notebooks are filled with observations and theories. One notebook is labeled "Lanulos," another "The Silver Bridge Collapse." There's a thick file folder for the "TNT Area," and a manila envelope labeled "Indrid Cold."

Among the papers, there are dozens of drawings of the Mothman, a seven-foot humanoid with wings and mesmerizing red eyes. Your grandfather has written the number 121567504 over and over and over again. It's scribbled in corners and margins. Sometimes it fills an entire notebook page.

None of it means anything to you, but your curiosity is piqued and you're eager to keep digging. That's when your eye catches on a half-written note:

If something happens to me go to the

Your grandfather's handwriting abruptly ends there. Your spine tingles. What was he trying to say? *If something happens to me!* What did he know about his own disappearance?

If you immediately take the important note downstairs to show it to your parents, turn to page 16.

If you continue to dig through the files and notebooks for more clues, turn to page 30.

121567504
121567504
1504
121567504

The basement.

You've been putting it off because it's creepy, but it's one of the last parts of the mansion you haven't yet explored. As you open the creaking door, a stale, musty smell wafts up the old wooden staircase. Huge moths flutter out, flapping past with their mushroom-colored, hairy bodies and long antennae. Your heart startles, but you can handle moths. It's giant spiders you absolutely don't want to find.

Shuddering at the thought, you squint down the stairs and into the abyss. Every horror movie you've ever seen flashes through your mind. A voice whispers inside your head: *Turn back*. You take a steadying breath, summoning another voice. A better one. *Be brave!*

Ahead there's a bare lightbulb with a chain attached. You pull the chain and the light blinks on. At the bottom of the stairs, you find more bulbs along the way, hanging from the low ceiling, creating a trail of dim, flickering light.

Go on to the next page.

There's an ancient washer and dryer. Shelves with old paint cans. And along an entire wall, a bank of metal file cabinets.

Curious, you open a drawer and find it stuffed full of documents. UFO SIGHTINGS IN AND NEAR POINT PLEASANT, WEST VIRGINIA. Another drawer is dedicated to something called THE TNT AREA. And yet another is crammed with hundreds of pages about THE MOTHMAN. You pull the file out and skim through it. Eyewitness accounts are handwritten in great detail. There's a thick collection of bone-chilling drawings. The Mothman is terrifying. A true monster. Seven feet tall, winged, clawed, and red-eyed.

Goosebumps spring up along your arms. Warily, holding your breath, you look over your shoulder, feeling a presence behind you. Your attention is drawn to a cobwebbed corner, where you catch a glint of something on the floor.

Turn to the next page.

Cautiously, you cross the room to find a pair of eyeglasses with red frames. You recognize them as your grandfather's! They're familiar to you from the many photos your parents have always hung on the walls.

He dropped his glasses down here . . . in a corner? That's odd. Had *he* been cornered? By someone, or something? The thought makes you shiver. After careful inspection, you decide there aren't any spiders in the ripped cobwebs. Grinding your teeth, you reach through the sticky strands, hoping a deadly black widow doesn't leap out and sink its fangs into your hand.

Thankfully, you manage to retrieve your grandfather's glasses without a spider bite. Breathing a sigh of relief, you grip them in your hand as you continue to explore the basement.

Soon you encounter a narrow crevice between the foundation's large, quarried stones. Most people would walk right past the gap, it's so small and hidden in the shadows. But you saw it!

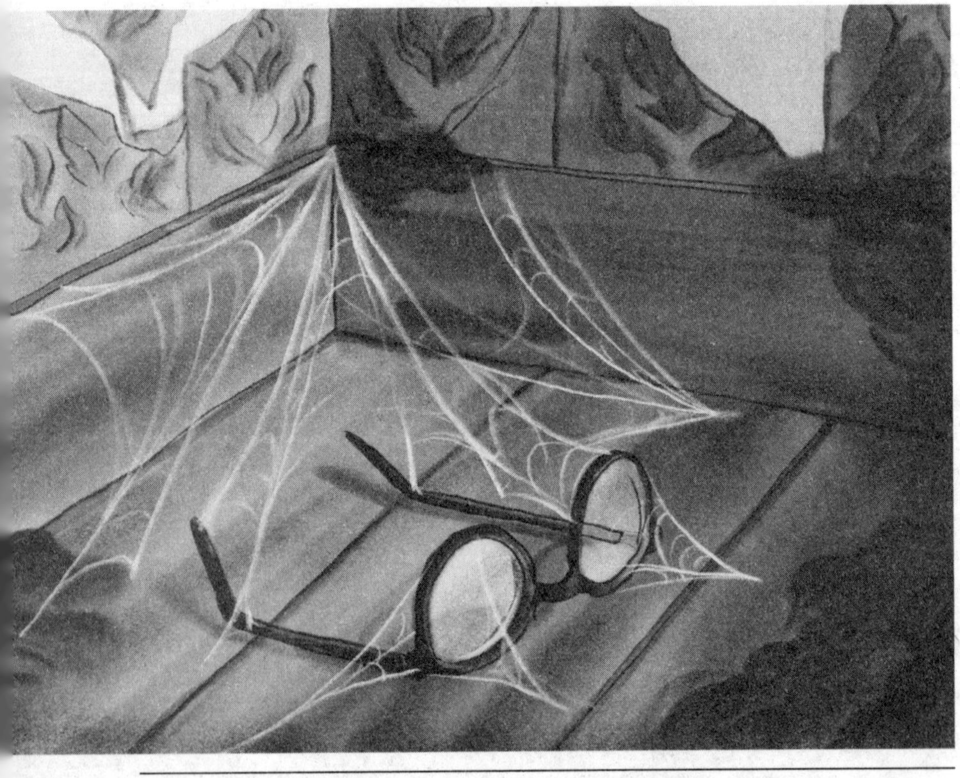

Go on to the next page.

As you stand at its threshold, your curiosity burns. *Be brave!* you tell yourself. Heart thudding, you turn sideways and squeeze through. Something hard bumps your head and you swallow a shriek.

It's just a lightbulb.

You let out a little laugh of relief and reach up to pull the chain. That's when you see something perfectly rectangular on the ground, covered with dust and pebbles. You reach down and brush it off with your hand. It's a sign with two arrows. Looking left and right, you realize the basement gives way to an underground tunnel system!

The left arrow points to AREA 15. If you choose this direction, turn to page 66.

The right arrow points to the TNT AREA. If you choose this direction, turn to page 90.

16

"Mom, Dad!" you cry, rushing into the kitchen.

"There you are," your mom says, smiling. She's holding a wrench in one hand and a hammer in the other. "Let's make the trek down to Point Pleasant. There's a festival today!"

"But I need to show you this." You thrust the note at them.

Your father takes it and squints. "Show us what?" he asks, handing it back. "Is that a phone number?"

You gasp. Your grandfather's half-written sentence has vanished! The paper is blank, other than the number *121567504* scribbled in pencil.

"I—I—" you stutter. "I don't understand. There was a note . . ."

"There are a million notes in this house. And diaries, and lists, and half-written novels," Mom says with a laugh. "Everything that popped into your grandfather's head."

"You ready to get some food?" Dad asks.

"But . . ." Your voice trails off again.

You stare at the paper, perplexed. You must have set your grandfather's note down on his messy table, and mistakenly picked up another. You'll have to go back upstairs and look.

Go on to the next page.

Later, though. Your stomach rumbles and festival food sounds delicious. Your parents are already heading outside to the car. You decide not to tell them about the secret office for now. It feels like your own special discovery, meant only for you.

Soon you're on the winding road down to the valley below and the sprawling Ohio River. Your dad points out a vibrant blue jay and a red cardinal, along with bright yellow wildflowers called goldenrod. A buck with a rack of antlers peeks out from behind the trees. The fall leaves are just beginning to turn orange and crimson.

When you park in Point Pleasant, you find tents lining the streets of the charming downtown. Live music plays. As you begin walking, the smell of corn dogs and cotton candy wafts through the air. Strolling down the sidewalk, you admire the old brick buildings, striped awnings, and cheerful fall flowers in bloom. A woman hands out flyers about a waterfront farmers' market, car shows, and revitalizing Main Street. "The future is now!" she says.

Turn to the next page.

And then you see the Mothman.

Right in the middle of the walkway.

He's a towering metal sculpture with veined wings, six-pack abs, and an insect face with mandibles. Below his feet (three claws each), a plaque entitled *Legend of the Mothman* describes the first sighting in 1966 at the TNT Area. You remember that your grandfather had a thick file folder about that place.

"Surprise!" Your mom spreads her arms wide. "This is the Mothman Festival! They have it every year. Fun, right?" She starts to dance to the music.

"Local legend," your dad explains. "There've been a lot of *supposed* Mothman sightings in the Point Pleasant area over the years." He rolls his eyes. Clearly, he doesn't share the same beliefs as your grandfather.

Go on to the next page.

It's then you realize that the vendors are all selling Mothman-themed merch: T-shirts, stickers, art, and books. There are advertisements for TNT Area tours. Lots of people are dressed up like the Mothman, too, with rubber masks and hairy socks and strap-on black wings.

It *is* fun, you have to agree. You can't help but smile.

"Meet you back here in fifteen minutes," Dad says.

Your parents hand you some money and let you explore on your own, while they stand in line for noodles. A few tents away, you buy a giant slice of pizza, and a chocolate cookie shaped like the Mothman with red candy eyes.

No matter where you turn, though, you keep seeing a man in a black suit. He's thin and pale, with oddly high cheekbones and a pointed chin. He's giving you the creeps. Finally, you duck behind a crowd of people and jog ahead. But when you look over your shoulder once more, he's still there.

He's following you, you're *sure* of it.

If you ignore him and go talk to a man about taking a TNT Area tour, turn to page 22.

If you turn and confront him, turn to page 74.

TOURS

MOTH FLOSS
TNT AREA TOURS

You ignore the weird man in black and head to a TNT Area tour booth where a cheerful bearded man greets you.

"Good afternoon!" His name tag says John Alva. "Care to join me for a tour this evening? I've got an opening with your name on it!"

"What kind of tour?" you ask. "What's there?"

"Ah! You must be new to this!" John says with a chuckle. "The TNT Area is where a bunch of abandoned World War II ammunition bunkers are hidden. But more importantly," he says with a wink, "it's where lots of Mothman sightings have occurred. Some folks believe that's where he lives."

"What do *you* believe?"

"I've seen some strange things out there," John replies, nodding solemnly. His bushy eyebrows come together. "Unexplainable."

"Like what?" you ask.

"You'll have to see for yourself."

Turn to page 24.

TNT
AREA
Tours
JOHN ALVA
MOTHMAN
TOUR

John wags a finger at another booth across the busy sidewalk. "Don't bother with my competitors. You won't see a dang thing, other than their own staff dressed up in costumes to spook you. Red flashlights and whatnot."

"They stage it all," you say, understanding.

"You bet. And they can't get to the remote spots in those big ole tour buses with their dainty little wheels. It's a muddy, rough mess back there! And it's a maze! I know the area like the back of my hand."

John proudly taps his own advertising poster. There's a photo of him driving a Jeep with huge, off-road tires. The words *we will finally glimpse the real truth* are written across the vehicle's hood.

A tour this evening sounds intriguing. Maybe you can learn more about your grandfather's obsession with the Mothman. On the other hand, John Alva's price is high, and you'll have to pay with your own allowance money.

If you decide it's worth the adventure and say yes to John's tour, turn to page 31.

If you politely decline, opting to rejoin your parents to check out the nearby Mothman Museum, turn to page 60.

“Don’t shoot!” you cry, throwing your hands in the air.

Within seconds you’re surrounded by armed soldiers. They’re wearing dark yellow uniforms, their arm patches decorated with odd symbols. You realize they’re stars connected with lines, like constellations. They spell out the letters I.M.

The soldiers confiscate your phone. “That way,” one of them barks, pushing you.

“No!” you cry, thinking he’s going to force you over the edge.

But just beyond the spot where you were spying, you see a gate. Concealed by a ridge of rock, it leads to a metal walkway. A soldier pulls out a key fob and waves it in front of a pad. The gate swings open.

Your hands held high in the air, you tremble as you zigzag down, down, down to Area 15. Your eyes itch and sting from your encounter with the Mothman, and the air grows cold as you descend. When you finally reach the bottom, you look back up in shock. You must be ten stories beneath the tunnel. It will be difficult for you to escape. There must be another way out.

Turn to the next page.

But before you can assess your surroundings, you're hustled past the saucer-shaped UFO and then forced into a small room. Inside, a man and woman in uniform greet you with silent nods. Their jackets are nearly covered with pins and patches. You can only assume they're officers, high up in the ranks. The door slides closed behind you and *clicks,* locking tight.

"What is this place?" you ask breathlessly. "What do you want from me?"

The uniformed man takes a step toward you, his eyebrows drawn together. "You've seen a Mothman."

"Yes!" you blurt. "In the tunnel. How did you know?"

"Your eyes. They're bloodshot from the actinic light of his red gaze," he says. "Don't worry. I can see it's a mild case. What's important is what you saw. Did you have a vision?"

Go on to the next page.

"I—I saw fire," you say, remembering. "A bridge blowing up. There were laser beams from an alien ship."

"Anything specific, like which bridge? A time, date, or location? It's critical that we know."

You shake your head.

"You *must* find out more," the female officer interjects. "We're running out of time. The evil Lanulans are orbiting Earth as we speak."

"Who?" you ask, confused. "What does this have to do with me?"

"This is Indrid Cold," she says, answering neither of your questions. She motions to a tall, thin man dressed entirely in black. You hadn't noticed him standing silently in the corner, which is unsettling since you're normally so perceptive.

"He's from the planet Lanulos in the galaxy Ganymede, and has been working with us, the I.M. The Intergalactic Military," she continues. "That's his ship you walked past. He's here as part of a peace envoy. He'll explain."

Turn to the next page.

"My home planet has survived a recent war," Indrid Cold says. His words come out slowly and awkwardly, and you realize he must speak another language on his planet. "There were two factions in the war. One wanted a society of countless species, including interplanetary residents. The other side wanted a strict two-race system on Lanulos, and to eradicate all others."

The I.M. woman in uniform interrupts. "The diversity side won the war. The bad guys are looking for a new planet to rule."

"They are coming to Earth," Indrid Cold says.

"To invade," the male officer adds. "With extremely hostile intentions. That's where you come in—we're hoping a Mothman will try to show you the future, a prophecy. They're known for warning people of future tragedies. Some people have the gift of communicating with them. They're seers. We think you're a seer, too. Will you help us?"

Go on to the next page.

A Mothman, not *the* Mothman. He's said that twice now, so it can't be a mistake. "There's more than one?" you ask.

"There aren't many left in the wild here, but yes," the woman answers.

"And what about my grandfather?" you ask, pulling his eyeglasses from your pocket and waving them in the air. "Where is *he*? Was he a seer? Did you ask him to do the same thing, to talk to a Mothman? And now he's gone! Why should I trust you? Why should I believe any of this?"

Just then there's a loud bang outside the door, along with panicked shouting. The door slides open and a wide-eyed soldier yells into the room, "Alien spies have infiltrated the facility!"

The two officers, along with Indrid Cold, rush out into the hallway. They duck and scatter as a blue laser beam bursts past, and a loud explosion follows. "That way!" someone shouts. The sound of their footsteps fades as they sprint away.

While everyone is distracted, you have the chance to make a run for it.

If you stay in the room and agree to help the I.M.'s mission to fight the evil aliens, turn to page 52.

If you decide you don't trust these so-called Intergalactic Military people and you flee, turn to page 79.

Overwhelmed by the amount of clutter, along with the questions swirling through your mind, your attention goes to your grandfather's antique desk. *Good idea*, you decide. The desk seems like a manageable project; it's relatively small with only a few drawers.

Besides, it's there that your grandfather grins at you from an old photo. He's wearing red-framed eyeglasses, standing alongside your parents, holding you when you were a baby! It makes you sad to know he's gone. You wish you'd spent more time with him when you had the chance.

The desk is beautifully carved from dark wood. You slide open a drawer and inside discover a leather box. You open it and find an impressive watch with multiple faces and dials. The watch's background is navy blue and looks like a compass, or a star chart.

You reverently hold the watch in your hands, deciding what to do with it.

If you wear the watch as a remembrance of your grandfather, turn to page 142.

If the watch seems too special and expensive to wear and you put it back in its box, turn to page 144.

The tour starts hours later, in the evening, so your mom drives you to the rendezvous point at the appointed time. After talking to some locals about John's background, your parents realized he'd been friends with your grandfather! So they decided they were okay with sending you off on your own.

You climb into the Jeep with John Alva and strap on your seat belt. Your mom eyes John skeptically, but in the end she seems satisfied.

"See you back here in an hour or so," she says, patting the hood of the Jeep and waving goodbye. "Have fun!"

It turns out no one else signed up for tonight's tour, so it's just you and John.

"Hang on!" John says as he abruptly turns off the cement street and onto a bumpy dirt road, which winds narrowly between ponds of murky water.

Turn to the next page.

Soon you enter the TNT Area, eerily peppered with igloo-shaped bunkers. They're perfectly camouflaged, built into the earth with bushes and weeds covering their roofs.

"You can't see these suckers from above," John says. "They're invisible. Which goes to show you it's all about perspective, kiddo. If you're flying overhead, they don't exist."

"These were full of ammunition?" you ask.

"From World War II," John says, nodding. "We thought they'd all been emptied out, but one of the bunkers went *kaboom* in 2010!"

"Yikes," you mutter.

"Bombs are the least of my concerns," John says gravely. "The Mothman is back."

Turn to page 34.

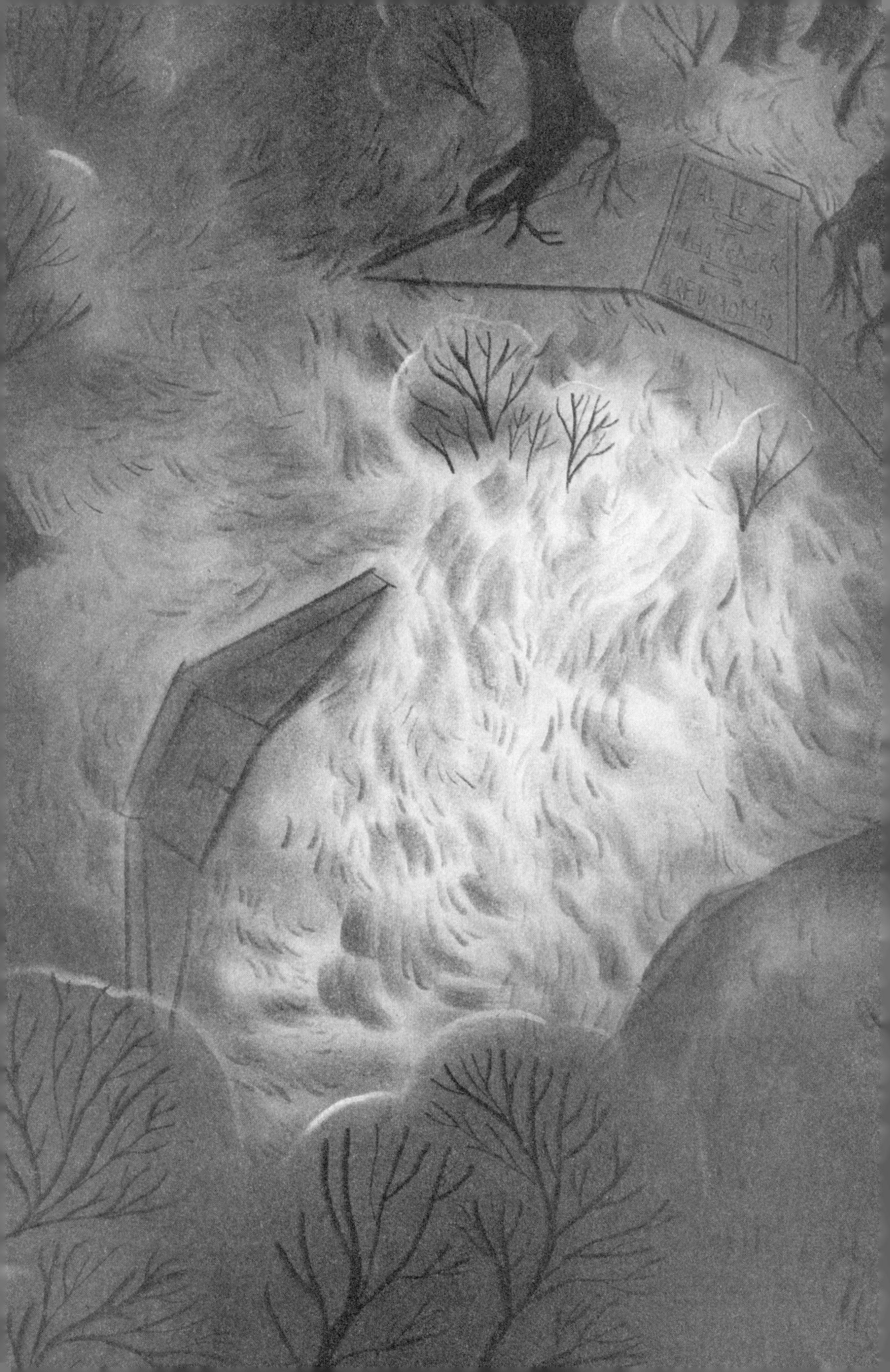

34

"There've been a lot of credible sightings over the past thirteen months. A lot of folks think he's trying to warn us about something real bad that's going to happen. You see, before the tragic Silver Bridge collapse back in 1967, the Mothman had been hanging around Point Pleasant exactly thirteen months prior. It was like he was trying to give people signals about the future, about what was going to happen." John turns to look at you, his thick eyebrows drawn together. "Your grandfather couldn't stop talking about his visions. Numbers. Explosions. I think they drove him mad." He lets out a heavy sigh. "I'm real sorry he disappeared. He was a good man."

Go on to the next page.

"I miss him," you say sadly, and then you both fall silent as you drive deeper into the woods. The rough terrain rattles your teeth. The sun has slipped behind the horizon. It makes you nervous that it's dark, but John believes—despite a few daytime sightings—that the Mothman is nocturnal. He explains that the Mothman is a type of cryptid creature, like Bigfoot and the Loch Ness Monster.

"Cryptids are excellent at hiding," John says. "In fact, the word *cryptid* comes from the Greek *kryptós*, which means *hidden* or *secret*. They don't *want* to be seen, which is probably why so many of them exist under the cover of darkness."

Turn to the next page.

A moment later, he grins and taps out a little song on the steering wheel. "Here! We! Are!" he announces, parking the Jeep in front of a shaggy bunker. "I believe this is the Mothman's lair."

"His *lair*?" you ask, getting out of the Jeep as he turns off the engine, leaving the headlights on. It's deathly quiet. A yellow moon is climbing. An owl hoots in the distance. Suddenly you feel an overwhelming sense of dread. Breaking into a monster's house doesn't seem like the best idea. It's not what you signed up for. "Is this safe?"

"As long as you watch your step," John says, pointing out giant, worm-like tree roots. You take in the graffiti ahead on the door—ALL YE WHO ENTER ARE DOOMED—and the poison ivy at your feet. That's when you notice a rusted, metal latch off to your left, hidden beneath the weeds. "What's that?"

Turn to page 38.

ALL YE
WHO ENTER
ARE DOOMED

"What's what?"

You kneel and push the leaves and branches away, careful to avoid the poison ivy.

"My goodness!" John gasps, dumbfounded.

You pull out your phone to turn on the flashlight, but the screen is frozen with snowy lines.

"Yep. Typical tech malfunction," John says. "Something up in space interferes with the signals. UFOs or whatnot. Some people think the government blocks them. Could be the Mothman, for all we know."

He flips on his battery-powered flashlight and shines it on the latch. "I've been out here a million times, and I've *never* noticed this latch." John gives you a wide grin, chuckling. "How did you even see it?"

Go on to the next page.

You shrug. You're not sure, honestly. You sort of *felt* it before you *saw* it. The same way you noticed the hidden doorknob in the hallway of your grandfather's mansion.

"I oughta hire you to work the tours with me, kid. Come on, this is exciting. Let's open her up!"

But you hesitate. Once again, you're overcome with an uneasy feeling deep in your gut.

If you open the hidden latch, turn to page 80

If you tell John you want to get the full tour and see the inside of the bunker first, turn to page 105.

It's a dungeon.

Musty and dark, this part of Area 15 is nothing like the high-tech shining floors above you. The scientist escorting you is a sturdy man with hair as white as his lab coat.

"Hurry along," he huffs, peering over his glasses at you.

Shivering with terror and anticipation, you slip on your grandfather's glasses, passing cell after cell. Inside each is a Mothman, crouched in a corner or gripping the metal bars with clawed, webbed hands. One swipe could kill you in an instant.

The narrow dungeon hallway twists and turns. There must be a hundred Mothmen, crowded into these miserable conditions. They shriek and hiss, your eyes catching on theirs, one after another. For just a moment at a time, you are swept into each of their minds, glimpsing their terrible visions of their own futures. Withering away in captivity. Never able to spread their wings and fly again.

"This isn't right!" you say, anger flooding your chest.

"They like the dark," says the scientist.

"They're in cages," you say firmly. You hadn't expected this. It's cruel. "They hate it!"

With a shudder of disgust, you realize the captured Mothmen are nothing but guinea pigs. Maybe you're a guinea pig, too! You're a part of some sort of government experiment.

"Where are we going?" you ask, noting that a few cells are empty, with their doors wide open. You hope you haven't been tricked. Is one of the cells meant for you?

"Number Seventy-Four," the scientist answers. "He's the most cooperative."

Turn to the next page.

Just glancing at these Mothmen has been hard enough. The idea of intensely locking eyes is horrifying. But you have to think about your grandfather. He's locked up in a prison as well—on a faraway alien moon! You must do whatever you can to save him.

Suddenly a man emerges from the far end of the narrow hallway. He's walking fast, coming toward you. The scientist tells you to pause by an empty cell to let him pass by. As he nears, you see he's wearing jeans and a gray T-shirt, and a green baseball cap that says *Tiny's Drive-In*. He's clearly not an I.M. soldier.

Go on to the next page.

He comes to a stop and stares at you with wild eyes. "What's going on?" he demands, pointing a finger at the scientist. "You're recruiting kids now? That's terrible, man! And listen! I don't want to do this anymore. I quit! I told you the numbers he gave me. It's the same every time. I'm not your Mothman telephone, dude! I refuse to be a pawn in your game!"

"Sure thing, Mason," the scientist says with a chuckle. He spins his key fob on his fingertip. "Exit as usual and your officer will debrief you."

You look past the scientist at the empty cell just behind him.

Here's your chance!

If you make a grab for the key fob and shove the scientist into the empty cell, turn to page 110.

If you stick with the plan and try to talk to the Mothman called "Seventy-Four," turn to page 121.

"What year is this?" you ask a woman dressed in plaid bell-bottom pants. She's standing next to her car, which is absurdly long, with metal fins running along the hood and trunk. It looks like the Batmobile.

"What do you mean?" she asks, sounding irritated. "It's 1967, of course."

Perplexed, you keep walking, passing a man in a truck hauling gravel. He pounds his horn. Someone complains that the light on the other side is stuck on green, and it's causing a rush-hour jam. You walk past more cars with frustrated drivers, pausing to talk to a gray-haired man smoking a cigarette with his window down. "Excuse me, sir. Where are we?"

Go on to the next page.

He gives you an odd look, but answers anyway. "This is the Silver Bridge." He points ahead. "That's Point Pleasant right there. Are you lost?"

Yes. Definitely lost.

You tuck your hands under your arms, wishing you had a coat, as the bridge itself seems to shiver. The tremor vibrates up your legs and into your chest, making your heart quiver with worry. Then suddenly, there's a terrible snapping noise above, like a horseman cracking his whip.

Turn to the next page.

46

The metal bridge cables are snapping!

Sparks fly into the night sky like fireworks, while all around you people scream. The bridge shrieks, too, as its metal frame twists. Bolts pop out and land at your feet where the cement is cracking and buckling. Soon, entire chunks break off and plummet into the water below, hitting the surface like bombs. You watch in horror as cars careen and flip off the bridge as the convulsing becomes violent.

"Too many heavy vehicles on this old bridge!" someone shouts as he runs past.

You try to run, too, but it's too late. Your foot catches on a fissure, and you trip forward and fall. But not to your knees. Not onto the road. No, you fall into thin air. The icy water of the Ohio River waits below. You twist your torso to grasp at a metal cord, but it slips through your fingers.

And as you fall, you see it. Perched high on the bridge, there's a huge creature with dark wings tucked behind its back. His red eyes blaze. The Mothman. He stares at you, straight into your soul, burning your eyes with his red gaze.

"Save me!" you scream as he takes flight. But he only circles high above, wings spread wide, watching your fates unfold like some sort of cursed angel.

The End

They're not numbers, they're symbols. No! They're letters in an alien language, some sort of military secret. *Lanulos*. You hear the words in your head. *Hurry*. The Mothman is warning you to be careful who you trust.

Frenetic, strobing images of destruction fill you with dizzy nausea. The beast looms closer with his ruby-red eyes. Your legs tremble. You feel weak, exhausted. You can't take it anymore. Beneath your feet, the bunker tips sideways. Darkness crowds your vision, and soon . . . there is nothing.

Turn to page 123.

50

You hurry toward the town, which twinkles with merry holiday lights. It's Point Pleasant, only it's different—like a version from an antique postcard, somewhere back in time. Carolers sing "Deck the Halls," and the festive mood cheers you, but only for a moment.

A terrible sound rips through the air. *Crack!* It's so loud you feel like your eardrums are splitting. *Crack! Crack!* You spin around to look.

The bridge's cables are snapping!

Go on to the next page.

You gape in horror as the bridge buckles. Chunks of metal and cement fall into the icy river below. All around you, crowds begin to form in the street, rushing out of the shops and restaurants to watch helplessly as vehicles plummet from the bridge and into the dark water. People are screaming and sobbing.

"Get some boats out there!" someone shouts. The crowd rushes around you, raging like an angry river themselves, flooding toward the failing bridge to see. Frantic voices overlap. "You can't jump in to help! You'll freeze to death! We need ambulances!"

It's more than you can take.

If you rip the cursed watch off your wrist, turn to page 156.

If you turn and run away from this heartbreaking nightmare so you can try to calm down and think, turn to page 177.

It feels like an eternity, but it's only a few minutes before the male I.M. officer and Indrid Cold return to the room.

"They've fled into the tunnels!" someone shouts in the hallway. "Four of them!"

"Four of who?" you ask.

"Alien spies," the officer says. He straightens his jacket and clears his throat, trying to compose himself. But you can tell he's upset. His voice is unsteady. "The situation is dire. Will you help?"

"I'll try," you reply warily. "But on one condition. Tell me where my grandfather is. What happened to him?"

"That's classified. Top secret."

"I need to know," you insist, feeling the heat in your cheeks. "Or I won't cooperate."

Go on to the next page.

"We can tell you he is alive," Indrid Cold offers.

"He's alive?" you cry, overcome with shock and joy. "Where?"

"Classified!" the officer barks at Cold.

"I am not bound by the same laws," Indrid Cold replies in his halting, robotic voice. "I can tell you. Your grandfather is in prison on a Lanulan moon."

You reel from this new piece of information. "In jail? In another . . . *galaxy*?"

"Yes," the officer confirms, giving Indrid Cold a hard look. He doesn't seem happy that Cold shared this guarded information.

"The only way to see your grandfather again is if you gather intelligence about the aliens' attack plans, and fast." It's the female I.M. officer, bursting into the room. She points at you. "Otherwise, nothing matters. Nothing! We'll be annihilated. You're our only hope. Will you communicate with a Mothman? Will you try to see the future?"

Turn to the next page.

"Where am I supposed to find a Mothman?" you ask. "Do you want me to go wandering around the tunnels again until I find one? There are alien spies in there now!"

"No," she responds. "We'll take you to one."

You consider the bravery you'll need to lock eyes with a monstrous Mothman again. You imagine his sharp claws, his towering height, his insect-like face. It sends a shiver down your spine. All of this is so hard to believe.

Turn to the next page.

"Fine," you finally say. "But I need something to protect my eyes from the actinic rays. I don't want to get burned again."

"You already have what you need," the man says. "Your grandfather's eyeglasses. That's what they're designed for. Are you ready?"

You nod. "For my grandfather," you say, pulling in a deep breath.

"For the entire planet," the man says grimly.

Turn to page 41.

The green door swings open and you stutter with disbelief. What lies ahead is hard to comprehend. There are cactus-shaped trees, but with veined blue leaves. The ground is covered in long, white grass, which bends in the wind. When you gaze up at the purple sky, you see flocks of Mothmen, flying majestically below the clouds. A bizarre creature perches on the crest of a rock, watching you with dark eyes. In a nearby lake, a monster rears its eel-like head before submerging again. You must have opened some sort of portal to another world, a universe of cryptids.

You're too distracted to notice when the door swings closed behind you.

You jump at the sound of the lock catching.

"No!" you gasp. You're still holding the key in your hand, but there's no slot for it on this side of the door. You're trapped!

The beast on the rock hisses at you, baring its giant incisors. Your blood runs cold. You have to run. You have to hide! As you sprint for your life, you realize the irony:

You're now the cryptid creature in this strange parallel world. And in order to survive, you must spend the rest of your days desperately trying not to be seen.

The End

12:15
N
S
W

Confident you've figured out the settings on the wristwatch, you twirl the miniature dials to the date your grandfather was last seen. Fastening the watch tightly around your wrist, you brace yourself for the dizzying ride through time. Immediately, though, your gut tells you that something is off.

You pause for only a moment, just long enough to see that you're still in the secret office. It looks neater, more organized. But then you're dizzy once again. Traveling again. You slow and pause once more, catching a glimpse of your grandfather. He's there, just across the room from you! He looks so young! You try to call out to him, but you're spinning faster.

It dawns on you that you cannot stop. You try to rip the watch from your wrist, but you've fastened it too tightly. It's too late. You're speeding too fast, too far, in reverse.

So far, in fact, you're nearly to the year you were born.

Time flies. In another blink of the eye, you disappear from existence altogether.

The End

Walking once again with your parents, the three of you soon reach a storefront with a bold sign on its window, advertising what's inside:

The World's Only Mothman Museum

"This should be fun!" your mom says, opening the door.

As you enter the museum, a friendly employee greets you. "Welcome!" she says with a smile. "Have a look around. I'm here if you have any questions."

You do, indeed, ask many questions about the history of the museum, the amount of supposed UFO activity in the area, and how the Mothman has been sighted several times over the past thirteen months. You find out your grandfather used to volunteer here as a tour guide!

Go on to the next page.

Actually, the museum reminds you of your grandfather's hidden office. It's full of information about the TNT Area, and famous investigators such as John Keel and Mary Hyre. You learn there was a major movie with Hollywood stars dramatizing the events of the 1960s, leading up to the collapse of the Silver Bridge. Glass displays showcase original newspaper clippings and handwritten eyewitness accounts of the Mothman, UFO sightings, and the mysterious Men in Black.

A few other patrons make their way through the museum, but there's a shifty guy wearing jeans, a gray T-shirt, and a green ball cap that says *Tiny's Drive-In*. Goosebumps spring up along your arms. For the second time today, you get the feeling you're being watched. Followed. You let out a frustrated sigh and do your best to avoid him.

Turn to the next page.

"Let me get your picture with the Mothman," your mom says.

"Do I have to?" you ask, but you go ahead and stand next to the replica, which is cheerfully smiling with its pointed teeth.

"Say cheese!"

"Cheesy!" you reply.

Turn to page 64.

She snaps a few photos before you move on to the gift shop, which is full of Mothman-themed books, posters, patches, hoodies, mugs, stickers, keychains, plushies, buttons, and magnets. You had no idea the Mothman had such a fan base.

Your dad hands you a bag. "I bought you a T-shirt!"

"Thanks," you say, pulling it out as you begin walking back to your parked car. On the front is a fluorescent green Mothman graphic with red eyes, its wings spread wide. On the back is a quote: *The universe does not exist as we think it exists. We do not exist as we think we exist. – John Keel*

It's a nice shirt, and the quote resonates with you. There are things that exist which we simply cannot see.

As you drive back to the house, you tuck the shirt back into the gift shop bag, finding something else inside. An envelope. You open it to find a ransom-style note! Mismatched letters have been cut from newspapers and magazines and glued onto the page. The letters spell out an ominous message:

stoP AskinG quEstiONs or Else!

Go on to the next page.

Your heart stutters. Is this threatening note meant for you? Or is it simply a marketing gimmick the museum puts in everyone's shopping bags? With all the displays about conspiracy theories, phone taps, and government cover-ups, it must be meant as a joke.

The gravel driveway crunches underneath the car tires as you approach your grandfather's house. Your dad twists around to look at you in the back seat. "Do you mind if we drop you off and continue up the road?" he asks. "We met a neighbor with a historic house who has some renovation tips. We'll be back in an hour."

"I think you'd be bored if you came with us," your mom adds.

"Sure thing," you say, closing the car door behind you and waving as they drive away, though when you look up at the towering mansion, dread sweeps over you once again.

If you call the Mothman Museum and ask about the strange note, turn to page 113.

If you continue to explore your grandfather's secret office, turn to page 114.

You snake your way underground, plunging deeper into the earth. Frustratingly, your phone is frozen with pixelated gray lines. The flashlight won't turn on. It buzzes faintly like a dying insect. Overhead, the bare lightbulbs become dimmer and fewer.

Your heart races. The journey feels endless. You've heard stories about people getting lost in cave systems. You're considering turning back when you abruptly reach the end . . . nearly losing your footing and plummeting straight into the abyss! One more step and you would've been a goner!

Go on to the next page.

After skittering backward to a safe distance, you gaze over the edge in awe.

Area 15 is a massive underground complex!

With towering metal structures stretching up and down a dozen stories, it's shaped like a cylinder, hollow in the middle. Elevators with clear shafts carry people dressed like scientists in lab coats, and soldiers in uniforms. High-tech panels cover the shiny walls.

From your hiding spot, you guess that Area 15 is run by the military. The question is—*whose* military? You don't recognize the mustard-yellow uniforms. Some troops wear helmets with eyepieces, making them look like they're out of a science-fiction movie.

Turn to the next page.

You carefully peer farther over the edge. In the center of the complex, an aircraft sits on a cement landing pad. But it's not an ordinary airplane, helicopter, or even spacecraft. It's a saucer-shaped UFO.

Suddenly you hear shouting. Soldiers! They're running with their weapons drawn. They're pointing up—at *you*! Oh no! You've been spotted!

Turn to page 70.

Adrenaline burns cold in your veins as you turn back toward the tunnel, ready to flee. But your path is blocked by a terrifying creature. The Mothman!

He's enormous, muscular, winged. Your legs wobble beneath you as you meet his glowing red eyes. Your own eyes burn as you spiral into a vision of fire. Green lasers from a spaceship are destroying a bridge. Chunks of cement along with cars drop into the dark water below. You're paralyzed with fear, trapped in the Mothman's mesmerizing gaze.

Behind you, you hear the soldiers coming, their footsteps stomping in military precision. You're trapped! But then suddenly the Mothman's eyes dim and you're released from the trance. Perhaps he was spooked by the soldiers and their weapons. He retreats into the darkness of the tunnel, lurking.

Gasping for breath, you feel your grandfather's eyeglasses in your shirt pocket, leaping with every heartbeat. You're sure you're on the right track to figure out what happened to him. There must be answers down in Area 15.

Suddenly, your stinging eyes are drawn to a narrow crevice in the rocks, and you realize there's another way. It's a passageway into an old coal mine!

If you hurry into the small tunnel leading to the old coal mine, turn to page 6.

If you surrender to the troops to gain access to Area 15, turn to page 25.

Your parents want to walk around a bit longer, but they're also eager to get back to their renovation projects. Soon, you're in your grandfather's secret study once again.

Try as you might, though, you cannot locate that mysterious note he wrote.

If something happens to me go to the

Go to the *what*? And where did you set down that note? You know you didn't imagine it! Frustrated, you turn your attention instead to the question of Indrid Cold, wondering if the pale man you met was lying about his identity. You locate the manila envelope labeled with his name, but it's empty! There's absolutely nothing inside, not a single scrap of paper.

You begin to wonder if things simply go missing from this room, as if by magic. Or—more likely—your grandfather took the contents of the manila envelope with him for some reason. If that's true, the information must have been very important.

Turn to page 30.

You grip the little knob, twist, and push the creaky door open.

Moths!

It's like a dark storm cloud. Hundreds, maybe thousands, swarm out toward you. Their dusty wings bat against your face. Frantically you duck and swat them away, trying not to shriek with disgust.

Finally, they've all flown down the hall, save a few clinging to the doorway. They're impressively large and hairy. Your parents warned you about finding "a few critters" in this house, like mice, rats, bats, spiders, maybe even racoons or squirrels. They explained that it would take a long while to get the old mansion renovated and totally cleaned up.

You remind yourself to be brave, but your heart isn't so sure. It pounds madly as you enter the secret room. Your breath catches. It's some kind of library or office. Sunlight streams through the cracked windows. The walls are lined with bookshelves. There's a leather couch and an old TV, a crusty coffeepot, a few dead plants, and a collection of telescopes. Three long wooden tables are pushed together in the middle of the room, covered with file folders, maps, yellowed books, and old newspaper clippings. An antique desk and chair sit in a corner.

Turn to page 10.

"What do you want?" you ask firmly. "You're following me."

"I know your grandfather." The man in black talks in a stilted, robotic tone, like he needs to think about each word. His fingers are strangely thin and long. On his wrist is an unusually thick watch with multiple faces and knobs. On his face are sunglasses, so you're unable to read the expression in his eyes, if there is any. He seems somewhat soulless.

"What do you mean you *know* him?" you ask. "He disappeared years ago, and everyone thinks he's dead. You *knew* him."

"He is still with us," the man says.

"Sure, okay," you say. "I know what you mean."

"Do you?"

"Yeah, he's in our hearts."

It's a thing grown-ups say to make everyone feel better.

But the pale man shakes his head. He points to a dog trotting past, a friendly-looking Labrador retriever on a leash. "Dogs hear things which humans cannot, true?"

Turn to page 76.

This guy is super weird. It's like he's from another planet. But there are hundreds of people milling around. It's not like you're alone in a dark alley—you can even see your parents from here, a little ways down the street. Plus, you want to know more about his connection to your grandfather, so you continue talking.

"Do you know what happened?" you ask. "Why did my grandfather disappear? Why was he never found?"

"You must answer my question first."

"Fine." You sigh, not understanding the point. "Yes. Dogs can hear higher-pitched noises."

"The noises exist, *even* if you, yourself, cannot hear them."

You nod.

Go on to the next page.

"There are also waves of light the human eye cannot detect. Nonetheless infrared and ultraviolet exist, correct?" He traces circles around his head with a pale, thin finger. "Invisible radio waves are all around us."

"What does this have to do with my grandfather?"

"Some people can sense things others cannot." He leans toward you, and you take a step back. Above his sunglasses, his thin eyebrows go up. "Some people can see. As can you?"

"Me? Oh, I, uh . . . I don't know what you mean," you say, though in your gut, you sort of do. You know you often notice details, things that other people miss. For example, the hidden door in the old mansion.

"You have answered my question," the man in black says with a maniacal smile.

"What's your name, mister?" you ask.

"I am Indrid Cold." He tilts his pointed chin at you. "I know what you are. I will see you in time."

Turn to the next page.

Indrid Cold. The name sounds familiar, but you can't remember where you've heard it before. Maybe in your grandfather's files? Yes, that's where it was.

"You didn't answer my question," you protest, calling after him. "What do you know about my grandfather?"

But he's already turned on his heel to leave. A long, black Cadillac with tinted windows pulls up to the curb. He slides into the passenger side and slams the door shut, and then the car zooms off.

Frustrated, you see your parents approaching.

If you ask to leave so you can go back to searching your grandfather's secret study, turn to page 71.

Across the street and a block away, you spot the Mothman Museum. If you head there, turn to page 182.

You race back to the center of the facility, darting behind the UFO to hide. Frantically, you look up at the floors above you, the elevators and countless hallways. There must be an exit door somewhere! A man shouts your name. Your heart freezes. They're looking for you!

The UFO's door is open! If you sneak inside to hide, turn to page 150.

If you sprint toward an elevator, turn to page 155.

John grabs the hidden latch and pulls it with a grunt. The small door swings open, revealing the start of an underground stairway.

"Unreal!" John breathes, grinning like a kid who's just unwrapped an epic birthday present. "My mind is blown." He flicks his fingers away from his forehead, making an explosion sound.

"You're welcome?" you say, still not sure this is a great idea.

It takes some effort to crawl inside the opening, then down the rough stone staircase. Ahead, the tunnel widens.

"Shh," John whispers, putting a finger to his lips. You've heard it too: a rustling. Something is coming. Could it be the Mothman? You tremble at the thought.

"Hide," John says quietly, tugging you into a recess. He flicks his flashlight off. You press your spine against the wall. As you hold your breath in the dark, you begin to wish you'd taken the cheap, cheesy bus tour instead.

Go on to the next page.

Something hurries past. It's hard to discern, but you think you see a wiggling tentacle! Two more figures rush by, speaking an odd, clicking language. You have no idea what they're saying, but they seem upset—perhaps that the latched door is wide open ahead, or maybe because they're fleeing something from behind.

You feel John shrink backward, but curiosity overtakes you. Slowly, slightly, you inch out to see.

Instantly, you regret your decision. Something thick and muscular whips around your waist! It squeezes painfully tight. You stop yourself from shouting John's name for help, so you don't give him away. Within seconds, you're thrust back up the stairs and through the door, and thrown onto the ground with a thud.

Turn to the next page.

82

You blink in disbelief and terror, taking in your four captors. They stand on two legs with humanoid torsos. Their heads are like killer whales' with shiny smooth skin and wide mouthfuls of small teeth. Instead of arms, a single tentacle protrudes from their alien chests, right in the middle. Two of them hold weapons, which you assume are laser guns.

Turn to page 84.

"P-p-please!" you stutter at the alien creatures. "L-let me go."

Instead, they force you through a densely wooded area, then up a hilltop. The clouds glow orange for a moment before a triangular aircraft lands. You have no choice but to board, and soon you're shooting silently into the atmosphere to rendezvous with their massive mothership. It's cloaked and invisible, revealing itself for only a moment as you fly into the docking station. You feel like a tiny minnow, floating helplessly into the mouth of a megalodon.

Shaking with fear, you're escorted off the aircraft and then into a shimmering gray room, where the walls seem to be made of fabric. You touch the surface, and it undulates but is solid. It's some sort of material that doesn't exist on Earth, and you realize that their technology is significantly more advanced.

Go on to the next page.

Finally, a single alien enters the room. Hunched over, with dull skin, it seems old. The door is still open behind it. But the alien is armed. "You see too much," it says in garbled English. You barely understand, but this must be their interpreter. "You go our prison. Lanulos moon colony."

Prison! On a moon colony?

"No!" you cry.

Desperate, you launch yourself at the alien. Its weapon clatters to the floor and discharges a rogue laser beam. The alien shrieks and crumples to the floor, milky white blood spilling from its octopus-like tentacle. It shot itself!

Turn to the next page.

This is your chance! You sprint down a hallway, soon discovering another docking station with an entire fleet of unguarded aircraft. You can see them through the clear floor. They hang off the bottom of the mothership like ripe fruit.

Escape pods!

You open a hatch in the floor and scramble inside. The door automatically slides shut over your head. There's a giant button on the control panel. You take a chance by pressing it, and it works! The pod disengages from the mothership and you jet off into space, leaving the hostile aliens behind.

Ahead, Earth glows brightly, a beautiful ball of green and blue.

But soon the pod goes terribly quiet. The engines seem to have stalled. The vessel suddenly lists sideways, and then begins to spin in circles.

The control panel is dotted with hundreds of buttons and levers labeled in a strange language you cannot read. The symbols resemble numbers, but backward and upside-down. Among them are two buttons that are much larger, so you figure they must be important.

You have to try *something. Anything*!

If you push the green button, turn to page 104.

If you push the blue button, turn to page 128.

Slow down and think, you tell yourself, trying to process everything you've seen up to this point.

You feel calm in your grandfather's office, you realize. You love being in this secret room, where you're surrounded by the knowledge he gathered over the years. He'd been searching for the truth. Your grandfather was onto something crucial. Is there really going to be an alien attack in the future? If so, how can you possibly stop it? There are answers here in these notebooks and file folders, you're sure of it. Plus, it's almost like spending time with him, and you miss him. His spirit lives between these four walls.

Regroup, read, and research, you decide. *Then* take action. The future has yet to be written. It can wait a day or two.

But soon you're hooked. Hours blur past. You spend every night sneaking in and out of the office, curtains drawn, door locked tight, combing through the endless books, notebooks, newspaper clippings, photos, and files.

Turn to the next page.

88

It begins to feel like quicksand, pulling you down. You aren't sleeping. You become paranoid. You can't trust anyone. Your grandfather's old TV occasionally buzzes and flickers to life, even though it's unplugged. Gray lines fizzle across the screen, emitting a series of beeping noises like Morse code. It's a message, you're sure! Someone is trying to communicate with you, but what are they saying? You can't figure it out. You sleep even less, vaguely aware this obsession is driving you mad. Is *this* what happened to your grandfather?

Meanwhile, your parents are so busy with contractors and electrical and roof repairs, it's a full week before they notice your bloodshot eyes and gaunt face.

You vehemently refuse to leave the house to go to the doctor's office. Finally, you're taken in restraints, kicking and screaming as you're hauled off to a medical facility. The staff medicates you to keep you calm, but it only enrages you further that you cannot access your grandfather's files.

The numbers! There's something important about those numbers! Mumbling "one two one five six seven five zero four," over and over, it's there in your stark white hospital room that you soon meet your untimely end.

The End

90

Steeling yourself, you follow the tunnel leading to the TNT Area. Judging by the volume of notes you found in the file cabinet, your grandfather believed it was important for some reason.

You reverently hold his lost eyeglasses in your hands, wondering if *he himself* got lost down here somewhere. Perhaps you'll find some clues.

Your nerves jangle with each step. The air is dank and smells of mildew. Eventually, the trail of lightbulbs ends. You continue ahead but are soon swallowed by darkness. Pulling your phone from your back pocket, you find the screen frozen in gray pixelated lines. It makes a low buzzing noise. You can't launch the flashlight. *Strange,* you think. And then you add *idiot*, angry at yourself. You should have thought to bring a battery-powered flashlight.

You'll have to turn back. But behind you, the trail of lightbulbs has gone dark, too! Heart pounding, you spin around at a sound—a fluttering noise. Now you're disoriented. Which way is back toward the basement?

Unfortunately, it no longer matters.

Horror chokes you as a pair of giant red eyes glow just ahead. Close, too close. In the inky dark, you see its wings unfolding. It's the Mothman! He's real, and hideous. You are keenly aware that you've startled him, and he's seething with fury. You want to run, but you're paralyzed by his red-eyed gaze. Your eyes burn and you see fire all around you. Flames scorch you. It's not actually happening, but it feels like it. It's some sort of vision of the future.

Turn to page 92.

You can't move. You can hardly even breathe, let alone scream for help, or beg for mercy. The Mothman hisses. He leaps. In your terror, you crush your grandfather's glasses in your hands as the beast's razor-sharp claws slash you.

Crumpling to the ground, you press your hands against your stomach, which is hot and slick with blood. Your guts uncoil through the gaping wound. As you lose consciousness, you spend your final moments wondering if this is how your grandfather also met his unlucky fate.

The End

Telling the truth seems to be a matter of life and death.

"Are you ready to talk?" the female officer asks.

"Yes. Here's what I know," you tell them. "The numbers 121567504 are import—"

"We already have that junk information." The male officer cuts you off, huffing impatiently. "It's the date of the Silver Bridge collapse. December 15, 1967, at 5:04 PM. It's something that happened in the past."

"Yes, those numbers are a dead end," comes a voice from behind you. You spin to look.

Turn to the next page.

"Indrid Cold from the Lanulan peace envoy, sir," a female soldier says, holding the door open for the man in black. He glides in like a ghost, pale and thin.

"Yes, of course. Mr. Cold needs no introduction," the male officer says, but he sounds startled, or perhaps confused. He stares at Cold. "Weren't you here with us in the room? I've asked you to stop disappearing without warning. You need to respect our protocols."

"Hello, Mr. Cold," you say.

"You know nothing of importance," Cold replies with a wry smile. His pointed chin is tipped at you as if he's aiming a dagger. His eyes are dark under the brim of his black hat. But you won't be intimidated. You've put the pieces together.

Turn to page 96.

96

"You're from Lanulos," you say.

"Yes."

"Then you would know they're *not* numbers. They're symbols in *your* language. What do they say?"

The male officer narrows his eyes at Cold. He pulls his broad shoulders back and straightens his military jacket, pins and medallions clinking. "Is this true?" he growls.

"He's not to be trusted," you say. "He's a traitor."

Cold suddenly pushes his sleeves back, revealing a thick wristwatch. He spins the tiny dials with his pale fingertips. "I will see you in time," he says, tipping his hat. His body blurs. He's disappearing!

But at the same time, both officers tackle him, ripping the watch from his wrist, making him solid again.

Go on to the next page.

"What is this thing?" the male officer asks, holding up the watch. Cold doesn't answer. "Some sort of spy device?" he presses. "You're not part of a peace envoy!" He gives his female colleague a heavy look, furrowing his brow. "We have to assume they're all double agents! Hold his spaceship and arrest everyone on it!"

Cold snarls at you as he's escorted from the room in handcuffs. You give him a cheerful little wave goodbye.

"Now that we know those numbers are meaningful, we can decode them ourselves," the female officer says, before rushing from the room. "Great work!" she calls over her shoulder.

"Indeed. Thank you," the male officer says, clapping you on the back. "I think we can safely assume you've just given the I.M. the intel we desperately needed. A crucial, missing piece of info. We can now crack the code, hack into the enemies' intelligence, and outmaneuver them before they attack."

Turn to the next page.

Yes, thanks to YOU and the Mothman, the Intergalactic Military has headed off a catastrophic alien invasion. You've saved planet Earth.

And as if things couldn't get better, you learn that your grandfather has been freed from an alien prison! He'd been held captive on a moon of Lanulos, one of the last remaining outposts of the evil aliens. They were finally overthrown, and he's been rescued.

For the first time since arriving in West Virginia and the Point Pleasant area, you feel the blanket of dread lift and float away. You feel light and free. Earth is safe. Your grandfather is coming home!

The End

“There’s nothing more to add,” you say, shrugging.

His face darkens. “We don’t believe you,” the military officer seethes. “You’ll be staying until you share every last detail of what the Mothman communicated to you. *All* of it.”

You’re whisked away to a stark room with a single metal chair and a thin mattress on the floor. A steady stream of officers and pale people in white lab coats come in and out of the room to continue their relentless questioning.

“What did you do with my grandfather?” you ask them in return.

The more they press, the less you want to talk. You’re only served one, cold meal a day. Your parents must be frantic, searching for you. Soon, what the Mothman showed you becomes a muddy smudge of memory. It feels completely imagined. You couldn’t tell your interrogators much now, even if you tried. In the windowless room, you sleep fitfully, fraught with nightmares. You’ve lost track of day and night. Soon, you refuse to say a single word. Everything is the same, the same, the same.

Turn to the next page.

100

Until a bearded soldier bursts into your prison-like room. "Come with me!" he shouts. He's red-faced and wild-eyed. "It's happening! And you're going to fight alongside us."

Fight?

He drags you along, down one corridor, then up another. Your legs are weak from your time in captivity. You're out of breath. Alarms blare. Uniformed, armed soldiers sprint past. Soon you're outside and the sunshine blinds you.

Squinting, you see a fleet of military vehicles with huge, thickly treaded tires. Hundreds of soldiers climb into them, engines roaring. The bearded man points you toward a platoon. Someone hands you a weapon so heavy you can hardly hold it. You feel faint with hunger and fatigue.

"Take this kid with you to the battle by the river," he says.

Battle?

Go on to the next page.

You're in no shape to fight. But you climb into the monstrous vehicle and rumble into downtown Point Pleasant. Though it is midday, the clouds flash with an uncanny shade of green, making them look bruised and haunted. You soon realize it's from the laser beams firing from black, triangular spaceships. Like a buzzing swarm of insects, there are too many to count. What's left of the bridge spanning the Ohio River dangles precariously. One more explosive green blast and it snaps in two.

Smoke billows through the air. The laser fire is deafening. You don't know where to aim your weapon. Hordes of orca-faced aliens march through downtown Point Pleasant, wielding weapons in their tentacles. People scream and flee. An out-of-control car crashes through the front window of the Mothman Museum. A woman sprinting past holds up her phone. "They're hitting us *everywhere*! The Brooklyn Bridge! The London Bridge!"

Turn to page 103.

With a sinking feeling, you know: The destruction will go far beyond bridges. The entire Earth will soon be ravaged by the invading aliens.

You set your heavy weapon down. You don't know how to use it anyway. Lighter without it, you try to run, hoping to get back to your grandfather's house. But you're too exhausted and weak.

You don't get far.

The End

104

The engines do not restart.

A shrieking alarm fills the small cabin, piercing your ears. Desperately, you try the other button, the blue one, smacking it again and again.

The entire control panel goes dark!

You feel foolish and angry at yourself. Of course you had no idea how to pilot an alien spacecraft! What were you thinking?

Dizzy with fear and the accelerating spinning of the escape pod, you can no longer see Earth. The blaring alarm drives daggers into your eardrums. Your eyes water. You wail from the pain, punching buttons at random. Gasping for air, you struggle to breathe. The oxygen levels must be running low. The cabin is depressurizing.

Soon a terrible force grips your skull as you spiral faster and faster into outer space. You're filled with regret. You should have accepted your fate and gone to the alien moon prison.

At least you would have survived.

The End

Heart pounding, you step through the moss-covered entrance. The old ammo bunker smells like wet cement and decaying leaves. It reminds you of the smell of a cemetery. Adrenaline floods your veins as something dark approaches . . .

Bats!

A swarm of black papery wings assaults you. You duck and swat, and as the creatures fly past, it sounds like they're whispering words in your ears. Almost understandable, but not quite, like shadows of speech.

"Those are *moths*!" John says with a gasp as the insects dart through the open doorway and into the night sky. He's right. They're not bats after all. "Black witch moths, huge ones!" he continues. "They're a sign of bad luck. Never seen them in a bunker before."

"What about spiders?" you ask warily as you step deeper into the bunker. Curtains of white webs drape the walls. They ripple under the weight of scurrying spiders. A lump of dread hardens in your throat. There must be thousands of them. Beneath the webs, fluorescent graffiti glows eerily in the beam of John's flashlight:

HOME OF THE MOTHMAN
DANGER! GO BACK!
KABOOM!

Turn to the next page.

106

"Hello?" you call out.

"What are you doing?" John says, shushing you.

"I don't know. This feels . . . *wrong*," you say, searching for the right word. "We're trying to sneak up on him. How would *you* like that?"

Breaking into the Mothman's home is a terrible idea, isn't it? You're an intruder. What will happen if you startle this dark creature? Won't he be furious? As you move deeper into the bunker, dread begins to take a chokehold on you. *Breathe*, you remind yourself.

"Shhh," John cautions, raising a finger to his lips as you round a bend.

Go on to the next page.

A pair of red eyes! They glow intensely at the far end of the cavernous space.

Your pulse quickens, but then you suddenly remember: John mentioned that the other tour groups use red lights to fake people out. *Okay, you got me,* you think, remembering how your dad rolled his eyes at the whole idea. Someone in a Mothman costume is probably about to jump-scare you. You've just wasted your allowance money on a silly tour.

But the unblinking red eyes move closer. Whatever they're attached to shifts in the darkness. It's big. You swallow a scream as a hairy-winged monster hulks forward. You know instantly: This thing is *real*. From its terrifying mandibles to its sinewy muscles, it's definitely not a costume!

John hollers, sounding hysterical. "RUN!"

Turn to page 109.

But you're mesmerized, pulled in by the Mothman's bottomless eyes. Inside their red centers is a riveting vision. It's so vivid, playing out like a movie. Fire, green laser beams, explosions. A bridge blowing up. The Statue of Liberty on fire! Numbers spiral past: 121567504. But somehow you know they're not really numbers . . . they're . . . .they're . . .

You lose the thread as hissing noises fill your head, then a whispering voice.

Indrid Cold, it says, rattling inside your own skull. *Beware.*

You should close your eyes. You should turn and run! But it feels like whatever the Mothman is trying to tell you is important.

If you stay locked in the Mothman's gaze, turn to page 49.

If you close your eyes to break the spell, then flee the bunker, turn to page 146.

110

You lunge for the key fob with one hand and shove the scientist with the other. A gun clatters to the ground, and you gasp with shock. He'd been armed! You kick the weapon away as Mason lets out a triumphant *whoop*.

"Yeah, little buddy!" he cries as he launches his weight against the scientist. The man grunts with surprise as he falls onto his rear, then slides to the back of the cell. Mason slams the door shut, then thrusts his fists in the air. "Viva la revolución!"

"You can't do this!" the scientist screams, scrambling to his feet.

"Karma, baby!" Mason says, cackling madly. He seems a little unhinged, probably from spending too much time down here with the Mothmen. It would happen to you, too, you realize. Sooner or later, your mind would unravel.

Mason points to the key fob in your hand. "That opens all the cells."

You nod, then run from one cage to the next, releasing the Mothmen. They skitter down the narrow corridor, their black wings folded against their backs. Mason sprints after them. "Freedom!" he screams.

You have one last Mothman to free. The one called Seventy-Four, named—you sadly realize—for the number on his cell.

Go on to the next page.

But when you swing the rusted door open with a heave, the beast doesn't move. Instead, he's statue-like, his hulking seven-foot frame cramped by the low ceilings. You take in his sculpted muscles, his insect-like mandibles. With a tremor of panic, you wonder what Mothmen eat. He snaps his gaze on you, staring intensely, his giant red eyes blazing.

And then, heart thrumming madly, you see. You see it all:

The invisible mothership uncloaks itself. It looms over an entire city. Thousands of smaller alien spacecraft pour across the sky, buzzing and swarming like flies. It's the invasion! The mass destruction.

And then you see a series of numbers. 121567504.

Turn to the next page.

Swimming in the Mothman's vision, you suddenly understand! They're not numbers! They're *symbols* in the Lanulan language.

The Mothman's eyes dim and you're released from his gaze. He lurches toward you. Gulping for a breath, you fumble backward, legs weak. But he only wants his freedom. The moment he's outside the cell, he hurries toward the exit.

If you take advantage of the chaos you've created and make a run for your own freedom, turn to page 79.

If you report what you know about the numbers to the officers in Area 15 turn to page 93.

If you're curious about where the Mothmen are going and you follow Seventy-Four, turn to page 166.

You find the Mothman Museum's phone number on the receipt for your T-shirt. Surely, they'll tell you that the envelope with the ransom-style note was just a surprise souvenir from them, meant to go along with the theme of the museum. You pull your phone from your back pocket and begin to dial the number.

But you're interrupted when your phone lights up with an incoming call. The screen identifies the caller as MOTHMAN!

You hold your phone away from you like it's a rabid animal about to bite. "H-hello?" you answer warily.

On the other end, there's nothing but a crackling grainy buzz. It sounds like the call could drop at any moment. A garbled, whispering voice says, "Fiiiiind."

"Find?" you ask, your heart skipping several beats. "Find what? Find who?"

"Aaaaattic." The guttural voice doesn't sound human.

"Who is this?" you ask, hands trembling. "Is this some kind of joke?"

The line goes dead. You immediately try returning the phone call, but you're met with a recorded message that says, "The number you have reached is no longer in service."

You turn and look up at the old mansion, its windows like dark eyes full of secrets.

If you head to your grandfather's office to continue searching for clues about his disappearance, turn to page 127.

If you decide to brave the attic, turn to page 148.

114

You settle into a chair at the long tables in the center of the room. Smoothing the threatening note out to analyze it, you wonder if your grandfather ever received anything similar. You'll have to search through his stacks of papers to see.

Your phone pings. It's a text from your mom telling you they'll be another hour.

Is that okay? Then we'll make dinner.

Take your time, you write back.

Time is what you need, because now you're wondering if the capitalized letters in the warning note spell out something important.

stoP AskinG quEstiONs or Else!

PAGE is all caps. So is the word ONE. Page one? Is this a clue?

Go on to the next page.

You look around your grandfather's office and immediately feel daunted. There are thousands of first pages in his books and journals. Where would you even begin? You stare at the note and wonder if it could mean something else.

Suddenly there's a loud *bang* and you jerk your head up to find someone bursting into the room! It's the guy with the green ball cap from the Mothman Museum! You were right. He'd been watching and following you. He followed you home!

Turn to the next page.

116

"What are you doing here?" you cry, springing to your feet. "Who are you? Get out!"

"Holy moly, what *is* this place?" he breathes, ignoring your demands. His eyes are wide as he takes in the file folders on the table, and the books on the shelves. "Your grandfather was hiding all this intel? Oh, man! If they find out, you're toast! They'll be swarming the place! They'll take you, too!"

"I'm calling the police," you say. "Stop touching things! Put that down! You can't just barge into someone's house!"

"I'm trying to warn you!" he yells, throwing his hands in the air. "Don't you get it? They're gonna come for you!"

"Who is *they*?"

"I told you to stop asking questions!" he says. "I'm trying to help!"

Go on to the next page.

"You made this note?" you ask, grabbing the paper and thrusting it at him. "What does it mean? The capital letters spell 'PAGE ONE.'"

He scrunches up his face. "I didn't do that on purpose!" Then he sucks in a breath and lets out a long whistle. "Whoa! You're just like your grandfather, trying to string things together. You've got a lot to learn, little buddy. Sometimes the dots don't connect!"

"You need to leave. Right now."

"Are you kidding me? Come on, let's get to work. We gotta burn everything."

"What? No! Never! There are clues in here about what happened to my grandfather."

Turn to the next page.

"I'll tell you what happ—" he starts, but the old TV in the corner begins to sizzle with static. The guy runs over to it and holds up the cord with the plug. "See? It's not even plugged into the wall! Don't you get what's happening? They're listening!"

He yanks some sort of weapon out of the back pocket of his jeans. It looks like a space laser gun from a science fiction movie. Before you can reason with him, he blasts the TV. It bursts into a ball of flame.

"Stop!" you shout, but the curtains behind the TV have already caught fire. The orange flames leap to a stack of papers, then the bookshelves. It all happens so fast. The smoke begins to choke you.

"Let's go!" the man cries, grabbing you by the arm.

Turn to the next page.

120

All you can do is run for your life, down the stairs and out the front door, as the house becomes an inferno. Your grandfather's research is lost. So is the strange guy. You catch a glimpse of him sprinting down the road, but you don't have the will to chase him. You're paralyzed with despair as you watch the mansion burn.

Answers turn to ash. You'll never know the truth.

The End

Mothman Seventy-Four bores his ruby-red eyes into you. Even with your grandfather's glasses on, his gaze is so intense it burns like acid.

I see the choices you make. His hissing voice rattles your brain. *My brethren and I deserve to be free.*

"Oh! No! I—I'm so sorry," you stutter, realizing your mistake.

And now I make the choice not to help you.

The Mothman spreads his magnificent black wings in the small cell, pressing against the tight walls.

If I will never fly again, I will let all of humanity die.

Turn to the next page.

122

You try to plead with him, but his eyes dim and he goes silent. He retreats to a back corner, into the shadows. Released from his spell, you glance at the scientist and groan. He's holding a weapon now, tapping it impatiently against his hip. The chance you had to grab the key fob is gone. Mason might have helped, too, but he's no longer in the dungeon.

"What did he tell you?" the scientist demands.

"I failed," you tell him miserably as he leads you back to the I.M. officers.

As you enter the room, the male officer nearly pounces on you. "Well then?" he asks impatiently.

Turn to page 99.

You wake up in a hospital bed. A doctor in a white lab coat stands over you.

"Hello," she says. "How are you feeling?"

Your eyes sting, but otherwise you seem okay, just very confused. You look around. "How did I get here?" you ask groggily. "What happened to Mr. Alva?"

"He is recovering at home. He does not remember anything," the woman says. She sits on a chair next to your bed and leans toward your face. Her skin is pale and her eyes are black. The way she talks is robotic, as if she's speaking a language she doesn't know perfectly. "We are very interested in what *you* remember."

We?

Turn to the next page.

Just then a man and woman enter the room wearing crisp military uniforms and highly shined black shoes. They hold their hats in their hands, nod at the doctor, then wordlessly stare at you. Their uniforms are an odd shade of dark yellow, like nothing you've ever seen before. You don't recognize them from the usual branches of the military.

"Can I go home?" you ask. "Are my parents here?"

"Our questions come first," the doctor says, patting your arm. Her hand is ice cold, her fingers oddly thin and long. "Tell us what you saw at the TNT site."

"I saw the Mothman!" you blurt. "He's real."

"Of course you did," the doctor says. "You have *klieg conjunctivitis*."

"What?"

"Your eyes were burned from the actinic rays," she explains. "From the light from his eyes. We have treated you medically. You will recover."

You gently rub your eyes, blinking to make sure your eyesight is okay as you scan the room for a wall clock. You begin to wonder if it's even the same day. The walls are bare, however. The room is practically empty. The doctor turns to look at the officers. Their expressions are stony.

Go on to the next page.

"Did he talk to you?" the man asks. Despite his gray hair, he looks strong.

You think for a moment. It's like trying to remember a dream. "Not exactly," you say.

The Mothman didn't speak out loud, but you remember seeing things deep inside his giant red eyes: a bridge blowing up, the Statue of Liberty on fire. You know that the numbers 121567504 aren't actually numbers. They're a military secret in an alien language. And Indrid Cold is not to be trusted.

"The Mothman communicated telepathically," the doctor urges. "Is that right?"

You pause. As ridiculous as it sounds, it does actually make sense. "I . . . I guess so."

"Tell us what he said," the military woman says. "It's a matter of national security."

"It's bigger than that," the gray-haired man adds grimly.

Turn to the next page.

You look around suspiciously. It's then you wonder if you're in a hospital after all. There are no IV bags or heart monitors or any other pieces of medical equipment in the room. You're not wearing a hospital gown. You're still in your clothes from the TNT tour with John Alva. The pale woman you presumed was a doctor isn't wearing a stethoscope around her neck, or a name tag.

"Are *you* Indrid Cold?" you ask suspiciously.

"Excuse me. I am needed elsewhere," the doctor says abruptly before leaving the room.

"How do you know that name? Indrid Cold. What did the Mothman say?" the military man demands, taking a menacing step toward you.

If you tell them the truth, turn to page 93.

If you decide you can't trust these strange people and you lie, telling them you can't remember anything at all, turn to page 99.

Back in your grandfather's office, you close your eyes for a moment and breathe, trying to get your bearings. Your instincts lead you to the old-fashioned desk. As you settle into the soft leather chair, a feeling prickles at you. You just know that this piece of furniture holds more than it seems.

Turn to page 144.

128

What have you done?!

The language flashing across the console screen is alien, but you can read the map. You've locked in a course for the galaxy Ganymede! Outside the cockpit windshield, starlight streams past as you accelerate.

You're frantically looking for a seat belt when a chamber glides up from the floor. An alarm screams at you with a rhythmic message. It can only be a countdown. You've seen enough movies to understand. It must be a cryosleep chamber, the only way to survive the hyper-speed journey across the universe.

Go on to the next page.

Reluctantly you climb inside the coffin-like chamber. The door seals shut, and you're immediately claustrophobic. A chemical mist fills the chamber, and you hold your breath, panicking and pounding on the door to get out.

But soon a deep calm sweeps over you.

Everything goes dark.

You wake up groggy and soaked with sweat. The cryo chamber is open, so you climb out and stumble to the cockpit windshield. Your ship is hurtling past an orange pockmarked moon toward a planet that resembles Earth, more green than blue. You wonder if you're still in cryosleep, because it feels like you're dreaming. It's hard to believe any of this is happening.

Turn to the next page.

Suddenly, a swarm of ships buzzes past your windshield, and you're enveloped in a bubble of light. You lurch sideways, feeling the tug on your little spacecraft. They must have caught you in a tractor beam! You've been captured!

As you helplessly pace the cabin, your mind races. What can you do to escape? Time is running out as your ship is guided into a landing station on the green and blue planet. All you can do is brace yourself for a fight.

But when the door opens, you're greeted by a smiling, bald man dressed in white. He looks human, except he has four ears. A woman—also bald with four ears—stands next to him, holding her hands out in a peaceful gesture. The man says something in a language you can't understand.

Turn to page 132.

132

"Welcome," the woman says. "I am his interpreter. He is our Gathering leader." She glances at a handheld device, then adds, "Gathering translates roughly as 'city' in your language."

The man continues to speak, and the woman chimes in with the translation. "Welcome to Lanulos. We have scanned your pupils and we know who you are. Please. You must be hungry and thirsty after your long journey. This way."

You blink in dismay. Lanulos is gorgeous. The trees are so tall they brush up against the clouds, which are pink like cotton candy. Neon-colored birds flit past. The buildings are so white and reflective you have to shield your eyes. Some are stained, though, with what looks like fire damage, and others have broken windows.

Go on to the next page.

"We are still recovering from the war," she explains. "Some work remains. I am sorry that they have found a new target in Earth."

"What?" you gasp. "What do you mean?"

"We are sorry to tell you the terrible news," the woman says solemnly. "While you were traveling in cryosleep, the enemy invaded your planet. You cannot return. Travel to Earth is too dangerous, and it is forbidden."

Turn to the next page.

"No!" you cry desperately, shaking your head. It can't be true. "I made a mistake coming here. I have to go home! What about my parents?"

"There is no way to know," she says sadly. "But we have good news for you. While the war here on Lanulos ended some time ago, we have finally defeated the heavily armed group on our primary moon. It was their last stronghold. Your grandfather was being held there as a prisoner. He is on his way to Lanulos as we speak."

Go on to the next page.

Your heart soars. You now have an answer as to what really happened to your grandfather, though it feels completely surreal. He's alive! You look up, wondering which of the spacecraft circling above might be carrying him to safety. At the same time, you think about Earth, beyond the clouds, so far away.

The Gathering leader says something, and the interpreter translates. "This is your home now," she says.

You nod, realizing you'll have to accept your fate.

Turn to the next page.

And so, alongside your grandfather, you enjoy a long, healthy life on the peaceful, lush planet of Lanulos. Their advanced technology allows your grandfather to live to the age of 168. You have children, grandchildren, and great-grandchildren of your own. The news about Earth is never good, and you mourn the life you left behind.

The End

138

Once outside, you gasp at the breathtaking view of the rippling Appalachian range and the trees tinged with fall colors. The porch is a cozy little space with a chair and a weather-battered rug. A tray sits on a small table, holding a teapot and cup. Your grandfather must have been out here before his disappearance, enjoying a hot drink while breathing the fresh air and listening to the birds.

But there are no birds singing.

It strikes you as odd. You remember that animals can sense if a predator is nearby. The woods will fall silent. It makes the hairs on the back of your neck stand up. You get the uncanny feeling you're not alone.

Warily, you look left, then right, spotting something attached to the roof. It looks like a giant perch. Clawed feet are curled around it! They're black and gigantic, attached to thick legs. Could it be the Mothman? You lean against the railing, straining to see the beast's body and face.

A sickening splintering noise breaks the silence. It's the rotten wooden railing, snapping under your weight! You drop the baseball bat, and then you plummet after it, arms flailing. Below, the brick patio awaits. The baseball bat snaps in half on impact.

Go on to the next page.

You're an inch from death when you hear the flap of wings and the snap of claws. Your nose grazes the bricks before you soar into the air, carried by the Mothman. His talon-like claws dig painfully into your sides. Choking for a breath, you're both terrified and exhilarated. You're alive! The treetops wave beneath you as you skim past their leafy heads. You hear birds singing once again.

After a long journey, you're deep in the mountains, tucked into the dark folds of ravines and hidden crannies. The Mothman dips and banks, and you're suddenly inside a cave, coming to a landing.

As you scramble to your feet, you're now able to see the mythic creature you didn't believe existed. The Mothman stands seven feet tall with a wingspan twice as big. His body is pure muscle. His eyes are red globes, which sit above his insect-like mandibles. You can't tell if he's covered in fur or feathers, but he's as dark as the cave's shadows. Trembling, you back away.

Turn to page 173.

140

Over the next week, you swiftly gain pride in your abilities, coordinating the communications between the Mothmen and Intergalactic Military. You are given the title of Ambassador, along with a new yellow uniform, which you wear with honor.

Because of your dedication and hard work, you end up collecting more information than the I.M. needs, helping them put the clues together to stave off the alien attack. If not for you, the Earth would have been invaded, and humans would have been decimated. The Mothmen would have lived in terror, biding their time until the aliens discovered their secret city.

As a bonus, you also pick up a great deal of the Mothmen's hissing language, which you find to be beautiful once your ear is tuned. Their focus on the present and future is inspirational, as you realize that dwelling on the past can be a negative choice.

Go on to the next page.

Once your duties are done and the Earth is saved, the Mothmen release you. You joyfully return home to your parents. But your life path has forever been altered. Your own future has been changed. Because of your uncanny ability to learn new languages quickly, you become an intergalactic translator for the I.M.

Over the course of your long and fruitful life, your uniform becomes heavy with medals and pins as you help negotiate peace treaties and avert wars across the universe. History will forever remember you as a hero of the galaxies.

The End

The moment you fasten the watch around your wrist, an uncomfortable pressure builds inside your skull. You blink, realizing the hands on the watch are spinning fast—in reverse. Then the entire room begins to flip.

Helplessly disoriented, you brace yourself. Everything is a murky, twisting blur. Suddenly the air is freezing cold. The spinning slows . . . then stops. Your ears pop and it takes you a moment to find your balance.

Where am I? you think.

Beneath your feet is a cement road. You're outside . . . at night . . . on a bridge! Below is a wide inky river. Snowflakes drift past. Your breath billows out in front of you as you gasp with disbelief. Across the way you can see a town decorated with festive holiday lights.

Go on to the next page.

You begin to walk among the vehicles on the bridge. No one is going anywhere. Traffic is stuck. Horns honk. A few people are out of their cars, trying to see ahead. Walking past, you notice the cars all look like old models, rectangular and low, trimmed with wide front grilles and whitewall tires. Everyone's clothes are dated, too. It's like you're in a movie from the 1960s.

The question isn't where, but when *am I?* you wonder, glancing warily at your grandfather's wristwatch.

If you ask someone what's going on, turn to page 44.

If you continue across the bridge to the town, turn to page 50.

144

You take a moment to admire the desk itself. It's a work of art. Intricate embellishments are carved into the wood. Among the flourishes and floral designs, however, you notice that one side is slightly different from the other. It's not perfectly symmetrical. In fact, one of the flowers curls into the distinct shape of an arrow!

The arrow points to a panel, so you press on it, already knowing it will pop open.

Of course you were right. There's a hidden compartment! Inside sits an ornate skeleton key. Breathlessly, you slide it out and hold it in the palm of your hand, wondering what it opens. But it only takes a moment for you to realize that the woodwork on the walls of the room holds more clues.

Go on to the next page.

After a few minutes of searching, you find another arrow! It's bigger, and it points to a wall panel that holds a framed piece of calligraphy.

cryp·to·zo·ol·o·gy
/ˌkriptəˌzō'äləjē/
The study of hidden (cryptid) creatures,
derived from the Greek word kryptós,
meaning secret.

Nerves thrumming with anticipation, you press both palms against the panel and lean into it. Instantly, it pops open with what sounds like a breath of relief, revealing a vibrant green door. Hands shaking, you fit the skeleton key into the lock and twist.

Turn to page 57.

"Look away!" John Alva screams in your ear. He grabs your arm, breaking the spell. "Follow me!"

"But . . . I can't see!" you cry, blinking madly. Your eyes burn as if they've been doused in acid. The intense red light of the Mothman's eyes must have seared your retinas. You squint into the darkness, barely able to discern the Mothman stepping out of the shadows, his giant eyes trying to latch back onto you.

"This way!" you hear John shout somewhere behind you.

Panicked, disoriented, you trip straight through a curtain of sticky spiderwebs. The searing pain is immediate as dozens of arachnids sink their deadly fangs into your face, your bare arms, and your hands. *Black widows*, you think hazily. A brown recluse bites your neck for good measure.

The last thing you remember is the sound of the Mothman's clawed feet scraping against the ground, its wings unfolding . . . and then John Alva screaming for mercy.

The End

148

You climb the stairs to the attic, nerves jangling. Was that phone call *really* from the Mothman? You let out a little laugh, trying to reassure yourself. Ridiculous, right? There's no such thing as the Mothman!

Nonetheless, doubt nags at you. What if there *is*? And why the attic?

The entire fourth floor of the mansion is crammed with dusty furniture, clothes, and boxes of *Star Trek* and *Twilight Zone* DVDs. *Stranger Things* posters are pinned to the walls. The air is hot and stuffy. You grab an old baseball bat to use as a weapon, just in case this is some kind of trap.

Go on to the next page.

Soon you find a fleet of telescopes lined up against the windows. Your grandfather must have spent hours up here gazing at stars and planets, contemplating the universe. A slight breeze sends a piece of paper with handwriting on it skittering past your feet. You realize that one of the windows is ajar. The rain has been coming in, damaging the floor. Another project for your parents to fix.

Before you close the window, though, you see it leads to a small porch outside.

If you go outside to the porch, turn to page 138.

If you turn to pick up the handwritten note, turn to page 163.

150

You jump inside the UFO. It's the perfect place to hide until the coast is clear. But to your surprise, Indrid Cold hurriedly boards behind you.

"Let us go to your grandfather," he says with an evil-looking smile as the door seals shut.

"W-what do you mean?" you stutter as two terrifying alien creatures emerge from an interior cabin. They have the faces of orcas and single tentacles protruding from their chests, and they snarl at you in a strange language. You wheeze with shock as one snaps a muscular tentacle around your neck, while the other sinks a needle into your arm.

Go on to the next page.

"Enjoy your cryosleep," you hear Indrid Cold say as you drift off into oblivion.

When you finally awaken in a cold sweat, you're on a thin mattress. Groggily, you pull yourself to your feet, feeling nauseated and disoriented. Outside your barred window is a barren landscape with pockmarked soil. It doesn't look like anywhere you recognize on Earth. The sky is orange.

"Thank goodness, you're awake!" a raspy voice cries from behind, startling you.

Turn to page 153.

You spin around to find yourself face-to-face with your grandfather!

"You're alive!" you cry, embracing him. He's so thin, he feels like he's made of paper.

"I hardly recognized you. You've grown up so much!" he says. "Look how tall you are!"

"But what are you doing here?" you ask, searching his hazy eyes. "Where are we?"

"On one of the moons of Lanulos. This is a prison! I was taken because I knew too much."

You reach into your pocket and retrieve his red-framed eyeglasses. "I found these in your basement."

"Oh," he says, gripping what's left of his white hair. "I'm so sorry. This is all my fault!" He takes the glasses and shakes his head furiously. "Stop asking questions. That's what they told me."

"Was it Indrid Cold?" you ask. "Did he abduct you, too?"

Your grandfather nods sadly. "Terrible creature."

Turn to the next page.

154

"Indrid Cold is a double agent," you say, putting the pieces together. "He infiltrated Area 15 to get top-secret information."

"Have hope!" your grandfather cries in his wheezy voice. "This little moon is all they have left. Any day now, we'll be rescued." He leans toward you, his bony hands on yours. He smiles. "Are you a Seer? Did you see things in a Mothman's eyes?"

"I did." And then a thought suddenly lands hard in your chest. "How long was I in cryosleep?"

"About two weeks," your grandfather says. "A bit more. It takes sixteen days plus seven hours to get here from Earth. Now, tell me about your parents. Where are they?"

You wearily walk to the window and thread your fingers through the bars. Did the hostile aliens attack while you were traveling through outer space? Could anyone else have stopped it?

Gazing out at the alien sky, blinking back tears, you can only helplessly wonder if the Earth is in flames.

The End

The number panel inside the elevator is overwhelming. There are buttons for twenty-seven floors! You can only assume many must run deep underground. Your mind races as you try to decide what to do. You were lucky enough to get the elevator all to yourself, but if you don't choose soon, the doors will reopen. You hear angry footsteps approaching. You'll be captured once again, and you have a feeling the I.M. officers won't be so reasonable with you this time.

If you choose number 1, hoping it's the top floor, above ground with a clearly marked exit, turn to page 159.

If you choose your lucky number, turn to page 161.

156

Hands shaking, you manage to unfasten the watch from your wrist. In your frenzied state, you accidentally drop it onto the icy cement sidewalk. You stoop to retrieve it just as a man's heavy steel-toed work boot crushes it.

The sickening *crack* tells you everything you need to know: Your fate has been sealed. You stare helplessly at the watch's delicate insides—coils and gears—its ruined guts. It reminds you of roadkill. The thought makes you want to vomit as you scoop up every last piece you can find.

But you know it's no use. Even if you were Dr. Frankenstein himself, you wouldn't be able to stitch the watch back together and jolt it back to life. It's dead. Which means you're stuck in the past. There's no internet. A bottle of Coke costs a dime. Neil Armstrong won't set foot on the moon for another two years. John F. Kennedy was assassinated just four years earlier.

Go on to the next page.

When you finally wander into the police station for help, you're afraid to tell anyone the truth. They'll think you've lost your mind. So you stick with the story that you have amnesia. You insist you only remember being on the bridge when it collapsed. Everything else is a blank.

After that, you become a ward of the state. A short time later, a kindhearted family adopts you and you start school, which is what leads you to the strangest thing of all:

Your grandfather is your classmate!

He's your age, in your grade. You can't stop staring at him in the hallways. He probably thinks you're oddly fixated on him, which is true. You look so much alike it's uncanny. He lives with his parents, who are of course your great-grandparents.

Turn to the next page.

But as soon as you graduate from high school, you move away. It feels like a bad idea to meet your own mother, and you know she'll be born soon. You've seen enough movies to know about disrupting the time-space continuum. You might accidentally erase your own existence. By now, you've become a loner anyway. No matter how hard you've tried to fit in, you'll always be different.

Eventually, you find success as a science fiction novelist, writing about all the technology you miss from the life you left behind. People think you're an eccentric visionary, a strange genius. You'll never be able to tell a single soul the truth. You become a hermit and spend the rest of your days in an isolated cabin in the northern woods. Some nights, when you walk alone, you catch sight of Bigfoot.

The End

The elevator shoots straight up like a rocket ship, making your ears pop. The floor numbers blink as you ascend, counting down. *Ding!* You've arrived at floor 1. Adrenaline pumps through your veins as the doors slide open. You're ready to run straight for the first EXIT sign you see.

But a woman in a white lab coat is there, blocking your way, as if she's been waiting for you the entire time.

"Hello," she says with a chilling smile. She stretches her arms across the doorway. "Indrid told me about you. You have seen the future through a Mothman's eyes, is that right?" She has the same halting voice as Indrid Cold, like she's not speaking her native language.

"Um?" you reply, not sure if you should tell her the truth. Over her shoulder, a floor-to-ceiling window lets in the bright sunshine. There's a doorway where people are coming and going. "I'm leaving now."

"Yes, you are. It is a tragedy," the woman says, making a *tsk-tsk* sound and shaking her head. She moves her right arm forward and now you can see she's holding a tiny laser gun. She aims it at your chest. "You are so young. But we cannot have you in the way of our plans to overthrow Earth."

Turn to the next page.

160

Her words make no sense. Your mind swirls with questions. You need to push her aside and run! But there's a burst of blue light. A burning smell. It takes a moment for you to realize what's happened. Dazed, you slump back inside the elevator. She reaches inside, pushes a button, and then strides away toward the sunshine. Light fades to darkness as the elevator doors—and your eyes—slide shut.

The End

Your lucky number has never failed you before. Crossing your fingers, you push the button.

The elevator zooms up, then sideways! You grip the handrails and close your eyes, feeling like you're on a carnival ride. Confusingly, you lurch down for maybe a half a floor, and then race horizontally again. By the time it stops, you feel like you've gone in a circle. You also feel like you might throw up.

Ding! The doors slide open, and you can't believe your eyes. You're back in your Grandfather's house!

Or at least, you think you are. You don't recognize this room at all, which looks like a cluttered and long-abandoned study. The walls are lined with bookshelves. There's a leather couch and an old TV, a crusty coffee pot, a few dead plants, and a collection of telescopes. Three long wooden tables are pushed together in the middle of the room, covered with file folders, maps, yellowed books, and old newspaper clippings. An antique desk and chair sit in a corner.

Turn to the next page.

162

You realize it's a shrine to your grandfather's obsessions. Scribbled in his shaky old handwriting, notebooks are filled with observations and theories.

Among the papers, there are dozens of drawings of the Mothman, a seven-foot humanoid with wings and mesmerizing red eyes. Your grandfather has written the number 121567504, over and over and over again. It's scribbled in corners and margins. Sometimes it fills an entire notebook page.

Turn to page 87.

You pick up the note and read your grandfather's shaky handwriting.

How the watch works is a mystery to me. I am lucky to have returned to the present alive after using it once. I am considering whether or not to destroy it. It is something like the Antikythera mechanism invented by Archimedes. I believe there are only two of these watches in existence. Indrid Cold wears the other. He uses it to explore possibilities in the timeline. I believe he is nefarious. He is intruding on the past and future in order to see how to best play out a plan. It is like one of those Choose Your Own Adventure *books. He goes back and forth in time to see which choices are best for his purposes, which will take him to his end goal of total success.*

But what is he planning?

If something happens to me go to the Intergalactic Military.

121567504

You read the note a dozen times, trying to make sense of it. Unfortunately, you won't be able to follow through on any of these leads. You smell the smoke before you feel the heat of the fire. When you try to leave the way you came in, you find that the steps leading downstairs are engulfed in flame.

Turn to page 165.

Desperate, you run outside onto the little patio. Orange flames snap out of the windows on the floors below you. Above, in a cloud of black smoke, there's something flying! Its dark body is nearly hidden among the billows of smoke. It seems intent on its own escape, flying fast and high toward the mountains.

As you cough violently, smoke fills your lungs. You have the choice to jump to the brick patio below, or wait for the flames to take you—along with your grandfather's house, and all of the clues within.

Unfortunately, it's not much of a choice at all.

The End

166

Mothman Seventy-Four is fast. For such a hulking creature, he's nimble too, squeezing through the dungeon's narrow passageways effortlessly. *Where is he going?* you wonder.

He's not following the route you took with the scientist down from Area 15. Instead, Mothman Seventy-Four has led you to a stone spiral stairway. He pauses. You freeze. Does he know you're behind him? You hold your breath, trembling. In the silence, you hear him inhale quickly several times, sniffing the air. Then he scrambles on. You quietly follow.

There's only one way now. Up and up and up. Your legs and lungs burn after so many steps, hundreds upon hundreds of them. Finally, you can smell what the Mothman must have earlier: fresh air! Soon, sunlight trickles in above you.

As you climb the last of the stairs, you're hardly able to stand. Your legs quiver from fatigue. And after being in the darkness, the bright light blinds you. As you squint, your heart sinks. The Mothman has surely flown off by now. You've lost him.

Go on to the next page.

But then suddenly, the sun dims. Something is blocking its light. You look up to see the Mothman looming over you like a storm cloud. His eyes glow red as he stares knowingly. You're a fool. You weren't quiet enough! Your labored footsteps and panting gave you away.

He spreads his giant laced wings and *hisses*.

"P-please," you manage before he leaps, grabbing your torso with his muscular arms and launching into the air. You kick your legs uselessly. You're flying! His taloned hands dig into your sides as you race above the trees and across the foothills.

After what seems like an eternity, you approach a towering mountain range and dip toward a Dracula-black castle, which is built directly into a ridge. The castle's façade is carved in the shape of pine trees. It's perfectly camouflaged in the wilderness.

You land and the Mothman forces you ahead. You shiver as you enter the formidable gates to MothTown.

Turn to the next page.

168

There are Mothmen everywhere, staring at you as you pass, catching you in their mesmerizing eyes, clicking their sharp mandibles. The stone alleyways are lined with small black castles topped with pine-tree shaped turrets. Their windows are round with red glass. Their doors are shaped like moth wings. Along the road, the lampposts are terrifying. The town seems to be lit with the eyes of dead Mothmen, which still cast an eerie red glow.

Turn to page 170.

170

Soon you are ushered into one of the castles. Mothman Seventy-Four leaves you alone, closing the winged metal door behind you. A moment later a creature emerges from another room. He has a bearded, craggy human face, but otherwise appears to be a Mothman.

"Welcome," he snarls. "I am Erebidae."

"You're . . . part human?" you ask.

"Half. My mother." That's all he says on the matter. Erebidae leans closer and you can see his very sharp teeth. "You are the chosen one. You must tell the humans of what is to come in order to save us all." He points a taloned finger in the air. "There is only one rule here. You must not speak of the past."

Go on to the next page.

"What do you mean?"

"In the Mothman culture and language, there are only three tenses. Present, future, and modal. What *is*, what *will be*, and what *may* or *might be*. To speak of the past is a high crime."

"All that hissing?" you ask. "It's an actual language?"

"Of course."

You think of the apocalyptic images you've seen in the Mothmen's eyes. They're visions of the future, things that are yet to come.

"But how are you supposed to talk about things that happened yesterday?" you ask. "Or last year, or—"

"—Silence!" Erebidae growls, spreading his wings menacingly. "There is no looking back. There is no regret. Your eyes are on the front of your head for a reason." He jabs a finger at you. "You will be banished if you commit this crime thrice."

Turn to the next page.

Banished, you think. "You mean I'll be released?"

He angrily flares his nostrils. "Are you ready to translate for the Mothmen? You will receive the information in the visions you are gifted to understand, and then you will transmit it to the Intergalactic Military through a messenger."

"And then what?" you ask. "I'm free to go?"

Erebidae glares at you. "We shall see."

If you cooperate, turn to page 140.

If you break the language rule two more times by speaking of the past, turn to page 174.

But his mesmerizing red eyes reel you in. You see yourself inside them. Spiraling visions of your future spin past, of what will happen if you leave his cave. You will be imprisoned on an alien moon. You will slip into an alternate universe. You will die in a mine. You will be shot by a blue laser. You will go insane.

Your eyes burn and blur, but the message is clear: You will stay. This is your home now. You will never leave this cave. The Mothman will not allow it. You will survive in hiding, deep within these mountains. Forever.

The End

174

"I should have never *followed* the Mothman," you say.

"Your second offense!" Erebidae growls. "I warn you. This is unwise!"

"You *said* I would be banished," you say defiantly, using the past tense for the third time. "I'll take that option. I'll find my way home somehow."

"Fool!" Erebidae cries. "You will be cast out, but not in the way you imagine."

Go on to the next page.

Your arrest is swift. You endure a strange court trial, and then you are sentenced. To ensure you never speak of the past again, your vocal cords are removed in a savage surgery. Your neck is scarred with a jagged red incision, which heals slowly with itchy lumps.

You are released from Mothman society, which simply means that you're treated as a criminal. You scour the city, checking every gate and passageway, but there's no way to escape their sealed mountain fortress. Over time, your back becomes hunched from looking at the ground in order to avoid eye contact with the Mothmen. Soon, you live in utter isolation in a tiny black castle, pacing the cold, stone hallways.

Turn to the next page.

176

You miss the sun. You miss your voice. You miss your parents. You miss pizza. The only thing the Mothmen feed you is rotten fruit.

And all you think about is the past. You are full of memories and regret. Your mind races in reverse. It doesn't take long for you to become feral. Your fingernails grow long and dirty; your hair is greasy. You're some sort of Gollum-like creature, wheezing in the shadows.

So by the time the invading aliens discover MothTown and laser-blast it into rubble and flames, you hardly even care.

The End

You run, desperate to get away from the bridge tragedy. Adrenaline floods your veins. The winter wind stings your face. You just need a safe, warm place to gather your thoughts and come up with a plan. Maybe you can find your way to your grandfather's mansion.

But your teeth chatter and your wrist aches terribly. Concerned, you look down at your grandfather's watch.

Oh no.

The hour and minute hands are spinning again, only this time they're fast-forwarding, whizzing ahead in time! Everything blurs and spins. You squeeze your eyes shut against the vertigo, until you finally slow and stop. It takes you a moment to regain your balance and clear your vision.

Turn to page 179.

Now it's a mild, cloudy day. Modern cars whiz past. You assume you're back in the present. But then you see a digital sign in front of the Point Pleasant Bank building. It cycles through the temperature, an advertisement for free checking, and today's date.

You're ten days in the future!

Your attention then snaps to another bridge spanning the river. It's not the same one as before, though. It looks newer, but that doesn't matter. It's about to fall too. You sense it before you see it. A dull vibrating sound shakes the air. Then thick green laser beams strike like angry lightning bolts. A black triangular-shaped UFO emerges from the clouds, drilling the bridge with lasers. Smaller ships buzz across the river like a swarm of giant flies. It's an invasion! Out of nowhere troops of armed orca-faced aliens stomp past on the streets. One of them sees you. It points a weapon!

Turn to the next page.

180

You're dizzy again—with terror and another crippling wave of vertigo. "Don't shoot!" you cry, as a blue laser whizzes hotly past your ear. Your grandfather's watch spins its hands, narrowly saving you, hurtling you through the days once more.

This time, when you open your eyes, you're back in his office, gasping for a breath. Your stomach roils and your mind races. *What in the world just happened?* You check your phone, which tells you you're in the present. Relieved to have returned safely, you wobble over to your grandfather's tables to search through his notes. The Silver Bridge collapsed in 1967. It's a fact of history. You must have gone back in time and witnessed it!

Go on to the next page.

But does that mean you also just glimpsed the future? Is there going to be a catastrophic alien invasion in ten days? If it hasn't happened yet, is there a way to stop it?

You place the watch back in the leather box where you found it, studying its miniature knobs and buttons. It's meant to be set and *controlled*. Of course it is! It will take you *where and when* you want, if you know how to use it.

After examining the array of settings, you decide they seem straightforward. There are longitude and latitude knobs for the location, along with changeable numbers for the date and time.

You begin to wonder if you could go back to the very day your grandfather disappeared and find out what happened. Maybe you could even prevent it!

If you carefully adjust the dials on the watch, setting it for the past to investigate your grandfather's disappearance, turn to page 59.

The past is the past, but the future has yet to be written. If you're more worried about a possible alien invasion, turn to page 87.

Motioning to the museum, you wave at your parents to follow. While you wait for them to catch up, you have a moment to think.

You decide to put the pale man out of your mind, at least for now. He was clearly out of *his*. Once you're back in your grandfather's office, you can read more about Indrid Cold and figure out if he really knew your grandfather after all. For now, you're skeptical.

Turn to page 60.

ABOUT THE ARTIST

Sofia Cavallari is an illustrator and author based in Rome, Italy. She grew up drawing dragons and dinosaurs and she now illustrates books for a living. She has a BA in Illustration and Animation and an MA in Communication Design, and she loves to read and illustrate anything with fantastical elements and a little mystery. She published her first graphic novel, *The Garden*, in 2022, and her illustrations appear in some of Rebel Girls' books and podcast episodes.

ABOUT THE AUTHOR

Cristin Bishara is a young adult author known for blending fantasy and science fiction. Her debut, *Relativity* (Bloomsbury, 2013), explores alternate realities, while *Vial of Tears* (Holiday House, 2021), inspired by Phoenician mythology, earned critical acclaim.

Bishara earned a Bachelor of Arts in English from Kenyon College and a Master of Fine Arts in creative writing (poetry) from St. Mary's College of California. Before venturing into novel writing, she worked as a freelance business writer, producing magazine articles as well as copy for gourmet food catalogs, advertisements, websites, and tourist guides. She has also taught composition and creative writing at the college level and in community workshops. Cristin is an occasional thesis reader for the Red Earth MFA program at Oklahoma City University.

In her spare time, she enjoys traveling, learning Spanish and Arabic, and cooking, especially her grandmother's Lebanese recipes. Cristin resides in Tampa, Florida, with her husband, two children, and two dogs.

A NOTE FROM THE AUTHOR

When I was a kid, I loved walking to my local library to check out an armful of books. I read a lot of *Choose Your Own Adventure* books, of course! Stories about Bigfoot were my favorites, too, and I became convinced that the beast was lurking in the patch of woods behind my house. I never saw his hairy face, but I've been interested in cryptid creatures ever since.

The word cryptid comes from the Greek, *kryptos*, which means *secret* or *hidden*. As it turns out, there are many types of these hidden animals, plus eyewitness accounts from people who swear they've seen them. You've heard of the Loch Ness Monster, no doubt. But what about the blood-sucking *chupacabra*? Or the Loveland frog-man, who wields a magic wand? Or the Florida Everglades' version of Bigfoot called a swamp ape, or skunk ape? The list of cryptid creatures goes on and on. If you'd like to find out more, you could start with the same books I did: *Tales of the Cryptids: Mysterious Creatures That May or May Not Exist* by Halls, Spears, and Young; and *The United States of Cryptids* by J.W. Ocker.

I also read *The Mothman Prophecies* by John Keel, which documents the history of Mothman sightings, the tragic Silver Bridge collapse, Indrid Cold, and the heightened UFO activity in the Point Pleasant area. *The Mothman Prophecies* movie was based on Keel's book and stars Richard Gere. (Ask your parents if you can watch it, since it's rated PG-13 and is a little scary.) There's also an episode on *Unsolved Mysteries* (season 4, episode 5) about the Mothman.

As I continued to dig into more research, I was surprised to learn that there's a devoted Mothman following. There really is an annual festival in Point Pleasant, just like there is in this book! If you want to go, it's usually the third weekend in September. And if you want a Mothman t-shirt, you can buy one from the Mothman Museum!

Soon, I had pages and pages of scribbled handwritten notes and ideas. It was time to put them all together into an exciting *Choose Your Own Adventure* story. Of course, I added my own creative spin and expanded the legends into something fresh and new, all while honoring the Mothman's history.

You might wonder how hard it is to plot a book with nineteen endings. Welp . . . I bought a huge roll of bright orange arrow stickers, and I compiled the book *on my wall* so I could see all the branches! (I got the idea from William Faulkner, who outlined chapters on his walls.) If you'd like to see what MOTHMAN looks like taped together on my office wall, check out my Instagram, where I've posted some videos that show my creative process.

Now that this book is done and published, readers like you have been asking: Cristin, do *you* believe the Mothman exists?

Hmm . . .

Do I?

As John Keel would say, "Belief has always been the enemy of truth; yet, ironically . . . belief can sometimes open the door."

READ THE SNEAK PEEK...

You had doubts about this summer job from the start. It's far from home, there's no Internet, and you're working for a university that always gave you the creeps.

"It's a summer camp!" your parents touted.

"In Antarctica?" you remember asking.

"Don't worry! We'll be watching your every move."

If only your parents had understood how strange that sounded.

None of this was what you wanted when you agreed to take a gap year. You thought that you'd be making your own decisions for the first time in your life. This summer was supposed to be *your* time to shine, preferably in the sun while drinking smoothies on sandy beaches. You're a certified lifeguard, after all, and you love swimming.

Instead, you're wearing your warmest socks and sweatpants because August is a winter month in these parts: the frozen continent, the crystal desert, the ultimate south.

Antarctica.

Fortunately, your job has perks. You've made new friends, the food is great, you spend all day playing games and watching movies, and the pay is *unbelievable*: $82,018.90 for working just six weeks as this camp's head counselor. In three more days, it'll all be over, and you'll fly home to collect your money—in *gold coins* for some reason—back in Arkham, Massachusetts.

But something's off this morning.

Turn to page 3.

As you rub your eyes, you wonder why you keep having headaches. Is it the lack of sunlight? The last time you or anyone saw the sun was when your airplane crossed the Southern Ocean. Since that was back in June, the last forty days have been one long lesson on polar night: a weird phenomenon where certain places go days, weeks, or even months without a sunrise.

The experience is affecting all the campers differently. In your case, you get headaches. Really bad ones, too. Especially at night.

And it's always night here.

Or maybe it's the constant whirring of computers. Your parents developed the AI that runs the camp, and it never sleeps. Your father bounced with excitement when he first described it to you: "Oh, you'll love BROTHR! It's so intelligent! It can upload itself onto anything and should help you through any problem."

Maybe that's the problem. Too much BROTHR.

Or maybe you just overslept.

You check your smartphone, sit upright, and leap straight into a hoodie.

The sweatshirt reads:

Miskatonic Summer Madness
Camp Starkweather, Antarctica

Turn to the next page.

4

"BROTHR! Turn on the lights!"

The room brightens with a golden glow from the floor up to the ceiling. It's supposed to resemble a rising sun and ease the mind—at least in theory.

"Good morning," the AI issues through your smartphone. "Did you sleep well?"

"No," you groan. You stumble over your belongings. With Miskatonic Summer Madness nearly over, everyone is packing. "Why didn't you wake me sooner?"

BROTHR hops to the television and then your laptop as you move throughout the room. "I'm sorry. I thought you desired extra bedrest."

"When I get *home*," you clarify. "I can't leave the campers on their own before then!"

"I understand. Please know Nurse Peters has a list of the status of all the campers and junior counselors for you."

"I know . . ." you say while trying to make sense of your hair. "What's the temperature?"

Go on to the next page.

"Negative seventy degrees Fahrenheit with a high of negative sixty-six degrees."

"*So* negative," you chide while slipping on a second pair of socks. "Is it safe to go outside?"

"Undetermined. The wind is fluctuating between twenty and fifty miles per hour."

"Will there be auroras?"

"Yes. Unusual solar activity will produce significant aurora australis."

"Good." You tie your boots. "I'll take the campers out to see them."

"Unadvisable. The forecast for today is cloudy."

"We'll see about that." You take your smartphone and dart out your door. As you hustle through the eating area, you find a smoothie with your name on it. "Thanks, BROTHR."

The words YOU'RE WELCOME display across the microwave as you leave.

If you visit Nurse Peters, turn to the next page.

If you hurry to the rec room, turn to page 9.

"Good morning," you greet Nurse Peters.

"Good *afternoon*," she playfully corrects. "How are you feeling?"

"Awful."

The nurse directs you to her table. "Dehydration again?"

"Whatever it is, I call it headaches."

"Mm-hmm. You and half the campers have it. Stick out your tongue and say, 'ahh.'"

You comply.

"Mm-hmm. Next time, please brush your teeth first."

"Are you a dentist now?" you ask, nearly swallowing the tongue depressor.

"No, but I'm thinking of joining the Space Force next semester. They need nurses too."

"Really?"

"Of course! In space, no one can hear your headaches."

Go on to the next page.

The nurse discards her stick. "You're fine. Just drink more water, and don't oversleep."

"Tell that to BROTHR," you groan as you slide off the table. "How's *everybody* else?"

The AI overhears this and displays their information on a nearby monitor.

NAME	**STATUS**	**TREATMENT**
ELEANOR	WELL	NONE
GUY	WELL	NONE
J.R.	[N/A]	[N/A]
JACKIE	EPISTAXIS	MONITORED (SOMNAMBULISM)
MOON	WELL	NONE
SAM	WELL	MONITORED (PTSD)
"SHEMP"	DELUSIONAL	[CLASSIFIED]
SKY	PARASOMNIA	THERAPY
TENDO	WELL	NONE

"Sky still has nightmares, Jackie has nosebleeds, and Shemp is still a handful," Peters explains.

Turn to the next page.

"So, nothing new?" you ask from behind your smoothie.

"Mm-hmm, and that's how I hope it stays. Just three more days of nice 'n' easy."

You finish your beverage, and Peters offers to toss the cup. "Thanks, nurse."

"Anytime, counselor."

You return her smile and approach the door. But before you leave, you ask, "Hey, Ursa?"

"Mm-hmm?"

"Why are you transferring? The pay's great here, and I thought you were one semester away from graduating."

The medical student pauses and goes rigid with her back to you. "BROTHR, exit the infirmary."

"Acknowledged," the AI answers, and the med lab darkens.

Peters turns to face you. "Between you and me, I suggest you stay far away from Miskatonic University. Particularly its School of Medicine."

You snicker. "I've been telling my parents that for years!"

"I'm serious."

Your smile fades. "Ursa, we're ten thousand miles away from Arkham. Isn't that far enough away?"

Your colleague considers this. "I'd rather be in outer space."

You ponder what she might mean by this as you make your way to the rec room.

Turn to page 12.

Camp Starkweather has hosted Miskatonic Summer Madness for . . . you honestly don't know how many years. Judging from the artifacts around you, Miskatonic University has maintained an interest in the station since at least the 1950s. Now that the school owns the building, Camp Starkweather's maze-like interior looks more like a museum. The facility is overstuffed with new technologies—BROTHR among them—alongside countless trophies from prior expeditions. Its halls are crowded with displays: crystallized gold from Mount Erebus, diamond-bearing kimberlite from Mount Meredith, dinosaur vertebrae and armor plates, pterodactyl teeth, seven different species of stuffed penguins, mummified seals, climbing gear from yesteryears, puukko knives, a makeshift flamethrower, and other oddities.

Turn to page 11.

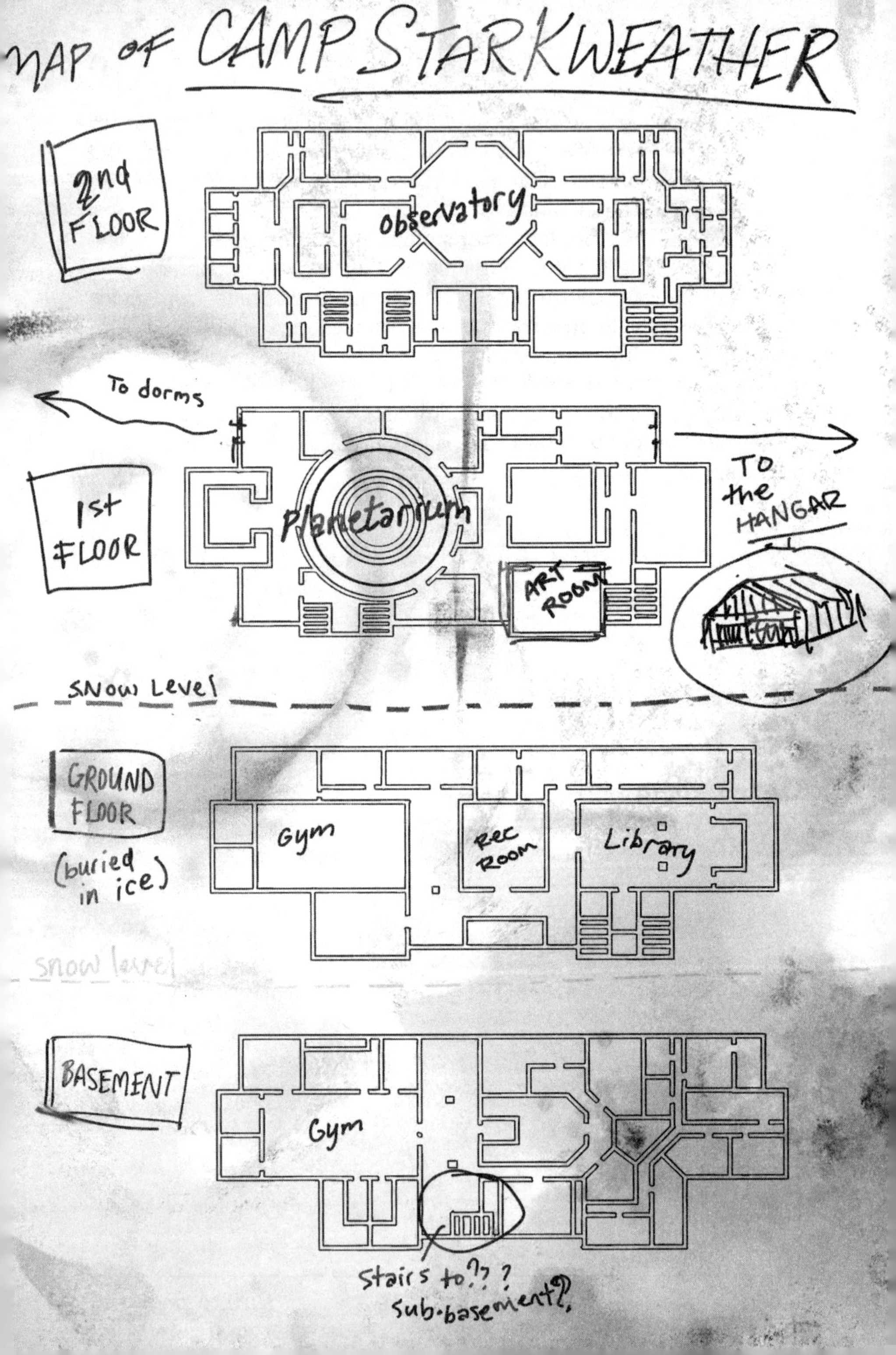
MAP OF CAMP STARKWEATHER
2nd FLOOR
observatory
To dorms
1st FLOOR
Planetarium
TO the HANGAR
ART ROOM
SNOW Level
GROUND FLOOR
(buried in ice)
Gym
Rec Room
Library
snow level
BASEMENT
Gym
Stairs to??? Sub-basement?

The exhibits made for great lessons throughout Miskatonic Summer Madness. But today, they're just a blur moving past you as quickly as you can run. The campers should be in the rec room by now, and you're already late to meet them.

As you pause to sip your smoothie, you once again fail to notice something on the wall. It's Dr. Septimus P. Olmstead, one of the creepy scientists your parents work with at Miskatonic University. The slender man's name is etched in brass beneath a photo of him with other professors during Camp Starkweather's early years.

If you turned your head, you'd notice Dr. Olmstead is the tallest person in the picture by several feet. Also, he's seated. And this photograph of him was taken nearly a hundred years ago.

With none of this in mind, you finish your drink and step inside the rec room for another fun-filled afternoon with happy campers.

Turn to the next page.

"Good morning!" you announce. "I mean, uh-oh . . ."

Half the campers point at you and laugh. An electronic clock beside you displays how very late you are today.

You smile and accept the ridicule. "I know," you sigh. "It's BROTHR's fault."

The campers laugh even harder and point at the clock, singing "*BOTHER!*" in a mocking singsong chant.

The clock goes from flashing "HA-HA" to "UH-OH" as BROTHR processes your insult. Humiliated, the AI quits the screen.

You smile and approach the heroes behind the camp's operation these last few months: its junior counselors. "Hi Eleanor, Sky. Sorry I'm late."

"We held the fort," says Eleanor, who everyone considers your second-in-command. You never offered her the title, and she never claimed it for herself. But she's smart, friendly, and the second-tallest person at the camp, so you never argued.

"Are you feeling better?" asks Sky, the older, shorter junior counselor.

"Not really," you answer. "You?"

The sleepless teen hides his bloodshot eyes behind his long blond hair. "I can't keep these images out of my head," he says. "I don't know what to do!"

"It's okay. Relax," you whisper calmly. "Did you try drawing them, like the nurse suggested?"

"I did! It's not helping. Look!" Sky hands you a detailed illustration of a *hyakume*—a fleshy, many-eyed monster from Japanese folklore. The blob-like creature is covered in eyeballs and stares menacingly at you.

"Wow," you say, impressed. "That's . . . truly haunting."

Turn to page 14.

CAMP STARKWEATHER
ANTARCTICA

14

Sky turns to Eleanor. "You see!"

The taller junior counselor smirks. "I'm still surprised how good that looks for someone who doesn't call himself an artist."

"But I'm *not* an artist!"

"Please lower your voice," you whisper. "Listen, Sky, I know what you're going through. This whole week has been one big headache. Why don't you take a quick nap in your room? We'll be fine. Just make sure you set an alarm for yourself. BROTHR will bungle it."

"Aye, aye!" Sky salutes you.

"Knock that off," you tell him. "This isn't Arkham Academy."

"Oh, yeah. I know." The junior counselor shifts anxiously. "Sorry."

"Don't sweat it." You offer Sky his drawing back.

"Keep it," he insists. "It'll help me sleep."

"That's the spirit." You smile. "Enjoy your nap."

Go on to the next page.

Once Sky leaves the room, you and Eleanor glance at each other and then at Sky's creepy drawing. "Seriously, I want a T-shirt of this thing."

"It looks professional!" she praises. "I like that snowy peak in the background. Do you think it's Fujiyama?"

"What?"

"Mount Fuji."

You study the illustration. "I think you're right! What an odd thing to remember about a nightmare." You roll the picture up. "I'm gonna do my rounds. Thanks for covering for me."

"Happy to," she returns. "And by the way, that *was* petty of you."

Turn to the next page

16

You smile awkwardly. "Are you talking about me and Sky? Really, I like him! I hope he gets into the Academy."

"I'm talking about BROTHR," Eleanor clarifies.

Your tone changes. "What about BROTHR?"

"Do you think it's wise to tease the machine in front of everybody?"

"BROTHR's AI. It has no emotions."

"Are you sure?" she asks you pointedly.

The words "HA-HA" and "UH-OH" suddenly flash in your mind.

"Remember that some of us depend on BROTHR for more than wake-up calls," your colleague cautions.

"You're right. Jeez, you're *very* right," you realize. "I'm sorry."

The junior counselor smiles and pats your arm. "Thanks for saying that instead of thinking it."

As Eleanor walks away, you consider her peculiar choice of words.

Then it hits you: "Uh-oh."

You glance around and wonder if BROTHR overheard your conversation.

You shake the thought from your head. It's just too weird.

Besides, it's time you checked on all the campers.

The adventure continues in
***At the Mountains of Madness*!**